BRAINWASH

A DANE MADDOCK ADVENTURE

DAVID WOOD
RICK CHESLER

BRAINWASH

Published by Adrenaline Press
www.adrenaline.press

Adrenaline Press is an imprint of Gryphonwood Press
www.gryphonwoodpress.com

Edited by Sean Ellis

ISBN-13: 978-1-940095-93-6
ISBN-10: 1-940095-93-X

"Angel's been kidnapped."

When Dane Maddock and Bones Bonebrake receive a disturbing message, the two former Navy SEALs set off in hot pursuit. They soon find themselves ensnared in a deadly game where the unexpected lurks around every corner and nothing is as it seems. With familiar enemies pulling the strings, can they survive the BRAINWASH?

Praise for The Dane Maddock Adventures!

"A great read that provides lots of action, and thoughtful insight as well, into strange realms that are sometimes best left unexplored." Paul Kemprecos, author of Cool Blue Tomb

"Dane and Bones.... Together they're unstoppable. Rip-roaring action from start to finish. Wit and humor throughout. Just one question - how soon until the next one? Because I can't wait." Graham Brown, author of Shadows of the Midnight Sun

"A non-stop thrill ride triple threat- smart, funny and mysterious!" Jeremy Robinson, author of Instinct and Threshold

"Ancient cave paintings? Cities of gold? Secret scrolls? Sign me up! A twisty tale of adventure and intrigue that never lets up and never lets go!" Robert Masello, author of The Medusa Amulet

BOOKS and SERIES by DAVID WOOD

The Dane Maddock Adventures
Dourado
Cibola
Quest
Icefall
Buccaneer
Atlantis
Ark
Xibalba
Loch
Solomon Key

Dane and Bones Origins
Freedom
Hell Ship
Splashdown
Dead Ice
Liberty
Electra
Amber
Justice
Treasure of the Dead

Adventures from the Dane Maddock Universe
Destination-Rio
Destination-Luxor
Berserk

The Tomb
Devil's Face
Cavern
Outpost
Arcanum
Magus
Brainwash
Herald
Maug

Jade Ihara Adventures (with Sean Ellis)
Oracle
Changeling
Exile

Bones Bonebrake Adventures
Primitive
The Book of Bones
Skin and Bones
Venom

Jake Crowley Adventures (with Alan Baxter)
Blood Codex
Anubis Key

Brock Stone Adventures
Arena of Souls
Track of the Beast (forthcoming)

Myrmidon Files (with Sean Ellis)
Destiny
Mystic

Sam Aston Investigations (with Alan Baxter)
Primordial
Overlord

Stand-Alone Novels
Into the Woods (with David S. Wood)
Callsign: Queen (with Jeremy Robinson)
Dark Rite (with Alan Baxter)

David Wood writing as David Debord

The Absent Gods Trilogy
The Silver Serpent
Keeper of the Mists
The Gates of Iron

The Impostor Prince (with Ryan A. Span)
Neptune's Key
The Zombie-Driven Life
You Suck

BOOKS by EDWARD G. TALBOT

James Robb Thrillers
Alive from New York
Alive from America
Alive and Worldwide

New World Orders
The Mayan Legacy

Dane Maddock Origins
Liberty
Justice

Dane Maddock Universe
Brainwash

Prologue

Minungo makes no sound as he creeps through the darkness back into the makeshift camp between the river and the trees. Nineteen summers in a clan which subsists by stalking animals to exhaustion has made stealth as much a part of his nature as breathing. Nevertheless, a voice stops him in his tracks.

"Is it done?"

Minungo turns his head to see a man with broad shoulders and slim hips barely visible in a pale sliver of moonlight. He is not surprised that Songo has detected his presence. The old warrior has seen more than fifty summers and possesses the senses of the gods themselves. There has never been any dispute about who leads the clan.

Minungo nods. "It's in their flames. Already they dance in the smoke."

Songo grunts. Minungo thinks he spots a trace of a smile gracing the chieftan's lips, but it could just be the flickering moonlight. Songo has long insisted that no fire be lit in the camps of his warriors, to better preserve all the senses for battle. Constant shadows merely add to Songo's aura of power.

"You have done well."

Songo pauses, then his voice grows huskier. "It is time."

Sixty minutes later, Minungo and Songo once again stand next to each other in the darkness. This time, light from a fire fifty yards away is visible through the trees. This time, they are accompanied by four dozen of the clan's finest warriors. To a man, they are armed with spears and curved nine inch daggers known as *chokwe*.

More than just a bonfire reveals the enemy to Songo's clan. A voice floats on the evening breeze, an enemy voice.

Is this not a bad idea? We will not be able to fight in these costumes.

Another voice responds.

There will be no fighting in this darkness. The costumes are the key. These are how we celebrate our power.

Songo motions to his warriors to creep closer. Soon Minungo sees the costumed enemy, elaborate headgear creating twelve foot shadows as they dance around a huge bonfire in a small clearing. Their movements are jerky from the weight and encumbrance of their attire. When Minungo was here earlier, the dancers had been completely without clothing. More voices carry on the wind.

Is this not heresy, to dress as the gods? Only the sorcerers may do that.

Have faith, my friend. This is how we HONOR the gods.

As Songo's warriors crouch on the edge of the clearing, the chieftain issues commands in a whisper.

"There are only two things to remember. First, you must strike immediately before they have time to fear you."

Songo's eyes scan the assembled warriors, their intensity a match for his gaze. The pause is long enough that Minungo can't stop himself from speaking.

"What is the second thing?"

Songo's grim countenance is one that could be worn by Death himself.

"Do not breathe the smoke."

Chapter 1

A tiny part of Bones Bonebrake knew that a third bottle of Dos Equis in the span of a single hour might be a bad idea. He acknowledged that part of himself by raising the bottle to no one in particular and downing it in one chug. The bartender turned at the sound of the empty bottle impacting the huge slab of driftwood serving as the bar.

"You all right, Bones?" The bartender, a tall, lean man with dark hair, looked down at him, concern in his eyes.

Bones shook his head. "I don't know, Mo. Lots on my mind."

"You don't seem yourself."

"I'll be all right, but you'd better switch me to Coke. Hold the Jack."

He looked around the bar, his eyes drifting past the many banners recognizing popular college football teams to the cluster that honored branches of the military, Special Forces, and POW-MIAs. Sloppy Joes was his favorite watering hole in Key West. Rebuilt after the Dominion had unleashed a freak tsunami upon the island, it still felt like the same old place. A bright, cheery spot where the staff knew and liked him… And also knew when to cut him off.

His gaze reached a tall blonde who was resolutely slogging through the sawdust between the restroom and one of the battered tables in the corner. He caught her eye briefly and raised his eyebrows, but she quickly looked away and sat down. He'd spotted her coming in half-an-hour ago with a corn-fed linebacker type wearing a wife-beater at least a size too small.

The linebacker grabbed her by the arm and sent a brief glare in Bones' direction. The girl's face twisted in pain. Bones cracked his knuckles and moved to the table with strides only possible for a man six-and-a-half-feet tall. The linebacker stood up as Bones arrived, but kept his fist wrapped around the girl's upper arm. He didn't quite match Bones' height even with the inch long brown spikes which passed for a haircut. But the shorter man had clearly spent a lot of time with both free weights and performance enhancing substances.

The man's face was halfway to crimson and toxic breath accompanied his words. "You got a problem?"

Bones' voice betrayed a trace of humor. "Let go of the girl."

"That's none of your business, red man."

Bones' grin widened at the slur on his Cherokee heritage. "Don't you know that's racist?"

The linebacker let go of the girl and started to poke a finger in Bones' direction. The finger never arrived. Instead, Bones redirected the finger, hand, arm, and shoulder behind the man's back. At the same time he slipped a foot behind one of the man's legs to prevent him from turning to relieve the pressure of the twisted arm. A quick move with the elbow over the man's neck and he was face down in his plate of French fries.

"Right about now, you're wishing you didn't use so much ketchup. Am I right?"

The unintelligible sound emitting from the table conveyed pain and anger. The man tried to lift his head, but a slight increase of pressure from Bones sent the message that movement would result in a compound fracture. He turned to the girl. "What do you see in this guy, anyway?"

For a second her face remained confused, then she stood up and glared down at the man. "I see an asshole."

Bones laughed. "Same thing I see. Do you come here often?"

The girl squinted at him and smiled. "Has that line ever worked?"

"Sure, when I use it after kicking the ass of the competition."

She giggled. "Fair enough. I could let you buy me a drink. But what are you going to do about him?"

"Him? What do you want me to do?"

"I don't know. It was our first date. Also our last date for sure."

Bones put a hand on each side of the carotid and squeezed. Within about ten seconds, the man had gone limp. He smirked at the girl. "Vulcan death grip."

Her eyes widened. "Quoting Star Trek? Don't tell me you're one of those crazy fans?"

"Hell no. Science fiction's not really my thing. Reality is much more interesting. Let me tell you about--"

Bones stopped as the door to the bar burst open, swinging around to slam violently into the wall. A well-built man with light blond hair stepped through. He seemed to bristle with intensity.

"Maddock," Bones groaned. "Hold on a minute."

Dane Maddock was Bones' business partner and best friend, though when they had had started out as Navy SEALS, the friendship had seemed unlikely. Years later, they had joined forces to become marine treasure hunters, and somehow they kept getting sucked into battles against forces which threatened to change the face of the planet.

He met his friend halfway across the room. "I know I'm hard to resist, but aren't you and my sister supposed to be off in the mountains somewhere?"

Dane Maddock's storm blue eyes were a Category Five hurricane, and Bones knew at that moment that any plans of getting to know the blonde girl better were out the window.

Maddock's words were a growl. "Angel's been kidnapped."

Chapter 2

Bones curled his fingers around the steering wheel of his Dodge pickup. "I'm going to kick their asses."

Maddock glanced over at his friend. Bones had removed the usual tie from his pony tail. His unfurled mane of long black hair made him look even more dangerous; almost savage. That was saying something, as Bones was one of the most dangerous men Maddock knew.

No one better by your side when things went FUBAR.

"No, you're not." Maddock replied. "Because I'm going to kill them. Slowly."

"Well, sure, but not until I kick their asses."

They both had a personal stake in the matter. Angelica "Angel" Bonebrake, was Bones' sister. The dark-haired beauty and mixed-martial arts champion fighter was also Dane Maddock's fiancée.

When she had failed to show up for their planned getaway to the Smoky Mountains, Maddock was concerned but nothing more than that. Calls and texts to her cell phone went unanswered. Ninety minutes after she was to have met him, Maddock received a text message with a picture attached, a picture of Angel bound and gagged with fear apparent in her eyes. The accompanying text read:

If you want to see her alive again, be at the bench on the Wildcat Ledge Trail in Shenandoah River State Park tomorrow at 9AM. No cops, no government.

Maddock and Bones had left their home port of Key West behind, and were now barreling up U.S. Route One. toward Miami. They had debated trying to catch a connecting flight from Key West, but driving to Miami Airport was the only way to get to Virginia in the time frame given by the kidnappers. Maddock found that he could barely contain his rage, which wasn't at all like him—

But it's Angel. They kidnapped Angel!

—and wasn't sure he trusted himself behind the wheel, so despite the fact that Bones was probably skirting the legal limit, Maddock had left his Bronco parked on the street, and let Bones take over the driving duties.

"Who do you think took her?" Bones asked, his tone uncharacteristically somber.

Maddock took a deep breath before answering. "Hard to say. We've pissed a lot of people off over the years. The Dominion. The Trident…"

Bones gave a harsh laugh. "Don't forget Grandma Ninja. She might be back in circulation, or spinning her webs from behind bars for all we know."

The Dominion and the Trident were organizations each bent in their own way toward finding historical artifacts of great power and controlling the world. The woman Bones had taken to calling Grandma Ninja was Edmonia Wright, a power-hungry octogenarian with mad kung fu skills.

"I haven't forgotten her. There's just no way to know until we get there."

Bones' fingers tightened on the wheel again. "You realize this could be a trap."

"Of course I realize that," Maddock snapped. He could feel his self-control slipping, and took another deep breath to calm himself. It didn't work. "In fact, I'm almost sure it's a trap. Doesn't matter, though. They have Angel."

"I hear you, bro."

The rest of the ride passed in silence, both men unwilling to voice their growing concern. Overhead, the black, velvet blanket of the night sky was broken by a massive full moon.

They left the truck in long term parking and headed towards their gate out near the end of Terminal E. The kidnappers had left just enough time for them to catch a midnight flight to D.C. At this time of night fewer travelers populated the vast airport, but Miami International was never really empty. A man rushing by them in the opposite direction managed to nick Bones in the ribs with an elbow, but by the time Bones had declared the canine nature of the passenger's mother, the offender was already ten yards away. He didn't look back.

Maddock put a hand on his friend's shoulder. "Save it for the kidnappers."

Bones shook off the hand, but there was no malice in the gesture. With a few minutes to spare, they dropped into a couple of empty seats next to the gate. Bones extended his palm to Maddock.

"Let me take a look at the message from the kidnappers."

Maddock handed over the iPhone, a recent acquisition he had made only at Angel's insistence. If it were up to him, phones would have remained tethered to wires in a wall. The big man navigated to the message with a deftness surprising for such massive thumbs.

Bones' face went still as he saw the picture. Then his eyebrows rose. "Are you even sure this is really Angel?"

"Of course I'm sure," Maddock replied irritably. But the question sprouted into a weed of doubt. He had more or less accepted the kidnappers' message at face value, and instead of demanding further proof of life, had simply gone along with their instructions.

"Did you try calling her?"

Maddock opened his mouth to tell Bones how ridiculous the question was, but then closed it without saying a word. *Why didn't I call her?*

He shook his head.

"She was supposed to meet you at five, right?"

"Yeah. We were going to crash somewhere

between Orlando and Tallahassee in the middle of the night."

"So why did you text her this morning to meet you at three instead?"

"What the hell are you talking about?"

Bones showed Maddock the chain of text messages from Angel. Sure enough, it showed a message sent from Maddock to Angel at 11:03AM:

Things are going quicker than expected. Want to get an early start and leave at 3 instead?

Maddock felt his face reddening. "I never sent that!"

"I assume you never saw the response, either?"

Off the boat early? U must really want 2C me. 3 is great.

Maddock shook his head. "I had the phone with me the whole time."

Bones sighed. "Dude, for a smart guy, you're not that bright. Whoever took Angel has some skills. They were obviously jamming your signal, which isn't a big deal, but they also managed to clone your cell phone to send the message to Angel. That's some NSA-type tech. But hold on a minute."

Bones brought up another screen on the phone.

"Looks like Angel set up the Find My iPhone app for you so you can see where her phone is."

The phone showed a map of Northern Virginia, with a phone icon and a green circle around it. Maddock stood up, fists and shoulders clenched.

"So Angel's phone is where they said she is."

Bones said, "Or maybe they've cloned hers also."

"Either way, we still have to go. But there are two other things we need to do. First thing is we need some specialized assistance."

"They said no government so I know you don't mean Tam. You're talking about a Wild Turkey drinking computer geek."

Maddock nodded. The "computer geek" to whom Bones was referring was Jimmy Letson, a former SEAL trainee who hadn't managed to make it through the rigorous program. Jimmy was now an investigative journalist, and a wizard with computers. He had helped Maddock and Bones many times before, asking only for copious quantities of alcohol in return.

"So what's the other thing we need to do?"

Maddock dropped the $700 phone onto the faded airport carpet, and then ground it under the heel of his left boot.

Chapter 3

The airport restroom was empty when Bones went in. The spot on his ribs where he'd taken the elbow shot had become increasingly tender, much more so than he would have expected from a glancing contact. The first boarding group was queued up, but there was still twelve minutes until the scheduled departure, and he wasn't sure when he'd get another chance to check. Besides, it would only take a few seconds.

He stopped in front of the sink, and allowed himself a grin as he gazed at his reflection in the wall mirror. Despite all the action he'd seen recently, he still looked like the same handsome bad-ass who had nearly killed Maddock during SEAL training all those years ago.

Good thing Maddock has mellowed out since then. I'm a good influence on him.

Remembering that he had only a few minutes, he quickly pulled up his shirt and inspected his lower torso. Sure enough, the skin was inflamed and puffy, tender to the touch.

It reminded him of the localized soreness he'd experienced after his last tetanus shot.

His eyebrows came together in a frown. Maybe the "bump" hadn't been quite so innocent after all.

He pulled his shirt back down and headed for the exit, eager to share this news with Maddock, but when he gripped the door handle and pulled, it remained firmly shut.

He pulled harder. Nothing.

A quick examination revealed that the door was locked, but no amount of force would rotate the bolt into the unlocked position. "What the—"

Somebody screwing with me? He wondered. *If so, they picked a bad day for it.*

He took a step back then drove his heel forward into the middle of the door. It might as well have been a solid block of concrete.

A chill ran through him as he considered the possibility that this was neither a harmless prank nor an accident. He turned and scanned the room. No windows, just the stalls, sinks, and a paper towel dispenser. He considered ripping the towel dispenser out of the wall and trying to smash in the door with it, but if a full-powered kick didn't do the trick, he doubted anything else would.

An idea occurred to him and he lunged toward the door and launched a kick at the wall next to it. His foot left a shallow impression, but failed to punch through. He grimaced when a jolt of pain went from his heel up into his lower back.

Concrete behind the drywall. Now I know. Should I try to yell for help?

His entire life of relying on himself told him to fix it himself, but then he remembered that his sister had been kidnapped.

"Maddock!" He shouted, beating the door with

his fist. "Maddock, You out there?"

Nothing.

A seed of panic blossomed. He intensified his assault on the door and began screaming.

"Help! Let me out! I'm trapped!"

He kept this up for a couple minutes and then stopped to put his ear to the door. He heard humming and vibration, but no sign that anyone had heard him.

The futile exertion had left him flushed and panting for air. He took a deep, calming breath.

Screw this, I gotta come up with something else.

His eyes went to the ceiling. There were a couple of crevices that probably held security cameras, and he gave each of them the finger. He also saw a smoke detector. He considered trying to disable it, which would likely set off some sort of alarm, but the ceiling was eighteen feet high and he couldn't see a way to get close.

He looked at his watch again. Eight minutes to go. He put his hand in his pockets, just to see if maybe he had something that could help. There wasn't much. To get through the security checkpoint, he'd put almost everything he'd brought along in his checked bag—along with his Glock, which probably would have come in pretty handy right now—but he had held onto his Mini Maglite.

That gave him an idea.

He tore the metal paper dispenser off the wall.

Kneeling on the ground, he set it with the open back facing upwards and removed all the paper. As quickly as he could, he tore the paper into smaller pieces and shoved them into the dispenser until it was about half full. He rushed over to the sink and ran a small amount of water into the nest of paper, enough to make it damp. Then he returned to the floor and filled the top of the dispenser with dry pieces of paper.

Next, he carefully unscrewed the cap of the flashlight and worked the bulb loose. Using the butt end of the tube as a hammer, he smashed the glass bulb, exposing the wire filament posts. He then reinserted the remains of the bulb into the socket, placed a piece of paper towel directly in contact with the filament, and switched it on.

Nothing happened.

"Crap," he muttered. "I really thought that would work."

He tried again and this time, the paper immediately ignited. Ignoring the flames licking at his fingers, he transferred it into the nest of paper in the dispenser.

The paper caught fire as well, and he let go of the foil. Within seconds, a healthy fire was burning. Soon, the flames hit the damp paper and it began to smoke.

He looked at his watch. Five minutes to go.

Waving the dispenser over his head, he positioned himself under the smoke detector. For several long seconds, nothing happened, but then, just when he was about to give up, the alarm sounded.

And the door lock snapped open.

Bones rushed to the door and sprinted back toward the gate. Strangely, nobody seemed to be reacting to the alarm siren. After a few seconds, the alarm fell silent. The woman at the entrance frowned and looked at her watch as he offered his boarding pass.

"Mr. Bonebrake? The door closes in thirty seconds."

Bones offered his best smile. "Just in time."

Under her disapproving gaze, he jogged down the ramp and reached the door to the aircraft just as it was starting to close. He ducked in past the surprised flight attendant and found his seat in the fifth row next to Maddock.

Maddock looked at him. "You must have really had to go."

"You have no idea." Bones closed his eyes and leaned his head back. He vaguely recalled that there was something he wanted to tell Maddock about, but couldn't for the life of him remember what it was.

Chapter 4

"**Maddock, far be** it from me to question the need for speed, but have you considered keeping it in double digits?"

Maddock had shaken most of the hyperbolic anger which he had felt in the hours after learning about Angel's kidnapping, replacing it with a deep and grim determination. Bones hadn't even tried to argue with him when Maddock insisted on being the one to drive the rented Camry from the airport out to the Shenandoah River State Park.

He glanced down at the dashboard. "I'm only going around eighty-five, Bones."

"Dude, that was fine when we were on the Interstate. Not so fine out here in the ass end of nowhere. I only bring this up because a speeding ticket would make us late."

Maddock eased off the gas pedal, but only slightly. He'd seen very few cars since trading I-66 for the two-lane backcountry Virginia roads, and he knew his limitations when it came to driving. He was anxious to get to the rendezvous, but Bones was right—it wouldn't help Angel one bit if they got rolled up by some local Barney Fife deputy intent on making an example of them.

The chirp of a cell phone curtailed further discussion on the matter. They had purchased a disposable phone from a 24-hour drug store after leaving the airport, and had only given the number to one person. Bones put the phone on speaker.

"You've reached the Love Connection."

There was a chuckle on the line, and then a nasally voice said, "If I have, then I've died and gone to Hell."

"Oh, it's you, Jimmy. I thought it was one of my many female admirers."

"You're a legend in your own mind, Bones. Now, are you interested in the info I tracked down or do you want to keep stroking your ego with dumb lines?"

"Lay it on me, bro."

"First thing is, some funky stuff definitely went down with Maddock and Angel's phones. That text from Maddock to Angel didn't originate anywhere near Maddock's phone. In fact, it originated from a tower near Bentonville, Virginia."

"That's where we're headed right now."

"Yeah. That lines up, I guess. There aren't many security or highway cameras in the area, not like in a city. I have my networks doing facial recognition on two or three I could find, but I don't have much hope of finding her that way."

"Thanks for trying," Maddock said. He had hoped for more, but Jimmy's talents relied upon the ubiquity of digital connectivity. It seemed that, even in the 21st Century, there were still a few places in America that remained well off the beaten track. "Let me know if you turn up anything."

"Not so fast. Shenandoah River State Park seemed like a really obscure place for a rendezvous, so I poked around for more information about the area, anything unusual that might suggest why the kidnappers chose that particular place. The park itself is fairly new—it was created in 1994—and comprises just 1,600 acres, which is a little smaller than Rock Creek Park here in D.C. It's a decent enough park, lots of amenities, but otherwise pretty unremarkable except for one thing. A few years ago, when the state park service was strapped for cash, they received a million-dollar anonymous donation to help them complete an infrastructure upgrade. Trails, buildings, access roads, etc."

"A million bucks and it was anonymous." Bones let out a low whistle. "Was it a bag of small unmarked bills?"

"Anonymous just means the donor didn't want his name advertised," Jimmy replied. Maddock could almost visualize him rolling his eyes. "But there's anonymous and then there's anonymous."

"Do tell. Who's the park's sugar daddy."

"I tracked it to a shell company in Wilmington, Delaware. That's not much help since there's about a million shell companies in Delaware, but I think I'll be able to follow the money to its source. But listen. If this anonymous benefactor is connected with Angel's kidnapping... Somebody who can drop a mil without even asking for a receipt for tax purposes is somebody with resources up the wazoo."

"Meaning?"

"Meaning, be careful."

Maddock glanced over at Bones. The big man

just shrugged. They both knew that they were way past careful.

Chapter 5

They arrived at the entrance to the park a few minutes later, continued up the drive passing the Visitor's Center, a low, brown building which looked like a thousand other park headquarters buildings around the country, and continued on to a campground parking lot not far from the beginning of the Cottonwood Trail, which led to the Wildcat Ledge Trail. They each removed a backpack containing various items which might wind up useful for a hike or a possible enemy engagement. That included weapons. They'd faced plenty of situations unarmed before, but Maddock couldn't think of a time when they'd brought along their guns and later regretted it. Maddock had his Walther P99, Bones a fourth-gen Glock 17, and both men had sheathed KA-BAR combat knives strapped to their calves. The weapons traveled just fine as checked luggage, unloaded and declared to the airlines.

There was enough shade that the morning sun didn't trouble them, although it was a humid August day. They came to a boardwalk, and shortly after that, the Wildcat Ledge Trail split off to the right.

As they made the turn, Bones said, "Any last thoughts?"

Maddock met his friend's stare. "We've done some crazy stuff, but usually we're better prepared than this. We're headed to a ground chosen by the enemy, with no idea what we're facing. They're probably watching us right now."

Bones made a face. "This is why you're no fun at parties."

Bones' attempt at humor fell flat as Maddock had already started up the hill. It took them less than five minutes to arrive at a bench overlooking the river valley. A strange mist shrouded the vista as they made their approach, but began to dissipate as they drew near. Maddock looked at his watch.

"We're early."

"Only ten minutes." Bones sat heavily on the bench, then turned sideways and leaned back until he was lying flat. "I'm gonna rest my eyes for a bit."

Maddock frowned. "You slept through most of the drive?"

"I know it must have seemed that way to you," Bones replied without opening his eyes. "But do you have any idea how hard it is to relax with you behind the wheel?"

Maddock shook his head. Every soldier knew how important it was to get rest when he could, and he knew Bones would be fully alert when the moment of truth arrived. He also knew that the big man's need to "rest his eyes" was just an act. Bones dealt with stress by making light of the situation.

Come to think of it, Bones made light of pretty much every situation, regardless of the stress level.

Maddock paced around the area, scanning the terrain in all directions as if surveying a battlefield.

For all he knew, that was exactly what it would become. He checked his watch again. It was 8:58 and there was no sign of anyone in the vicinity. He was about to share this observation with Bones when he noticed something underneath the bench.

"Bones, what is that?"

Bones opened his eyes and followed the line of Maddock's pointed finger. He reached under the bench and brought up a canvas package about an inch thick and a foot on each side. He tore it open and extracted the sole item contained inside. "Huh."

By now, Maddock was next to Bones looking at the discovery. "An iPhone," he remarked.

Bones nodded. "Nice one, too. Better than that piece of crap Angel bought for you." He winced almost as soon as he said his sister's name, then shrugged it off and thumbed the power button. A GPS map application was running.

"What the hell?" Bones murmured. "They think we're lost?"

"There's a pinned location," Maddock said, taking the phone and zooming out until he could see the orientation of the pin and the arrow that marked their present location. "It's about 400 meters northwest of here. I guess that's where we're supposed to go."

Bones peered in that direction. "Doesn't look like we can get there from here."

Maddock followed his friend's gaze and saw a steep rock face in the indicated direction. "Come on," he chided. "We can handle that. It's barely a scramble and I know you're almost as good a climber as I am."

Bones scowled, though it didn't extend to his eyes. "In your dreams, little man."

Maddock grinned but the levity quickly left his face. "Anyway, it doesn't look like we have much of a choice."

He was about to put the phone away when it started trilling and vibrating in his hand. He stared at the screen and the message "Incoming Facetime video call."

Maddock exchanged a wary glance with Bones, then hit the "Accept" button.

A live video filled the screen, the image jumping crazily as the camera—presumably integrated into a phone or tablet computer—shifted position. When it settled after a moment, it revealed the familiar figure of Angel Bonebrake, bound and gagged in a nondescript chair in an otherwise blank room. The camera lingered on her only for a few seconds before jumping again. When the image resolved again, it showed a vaguely man-shaped outline—the face was a pixilated blur. The figure spoke, the voice electronically distorted to further mask the identity of the kidnapper.

"Maddock. Punctual as expected. I see you brought your sidekick along."

"Who the hell are you calling 'sidekick'?" Bones snapped.

"Simmer down, little Hiawatha. Your sister's life depends on you listening carefully. Now, do I have your attention?"

"If you hurt one hair on her head," Maddock growled, "You'll have my complete undivided attention for the rest of your short life."

"Nice," the anonymous caller said. "Let's waste what little time she has left with macho chest thumping."

With an effort, Maddock brought his anger under control. "What do you want?"

"I want you two to do what you do best. Find something that's been lost for a very long time."

Maddock and Bones exchanged a glance. The request was unexpected, though it made a lot of sense. He and Bones didn't have a lot of money for a ransom, but their expertise was unique and invaluable. "What? Exactly?"

"Good. Now you're asking the right questions." The kidnapper paused a beat. "Listen carefully because I won't repeat this.

"In 1942, shortly after the Japs attacked Pearl Harbor, the Secret Service began transferring important documents and other items of historical significance to secure vaults hidden in remote locations."

Maddock nodded absently. He'd read about the temporary relocation of the Constitution, the Declaration of Independence, and other irreplaceable books and documents, but had no idea what any of that had to do with him.

"Many of those national treasures—" The distorted voice lingered over the description, as if trying to convey irony. "—were stored at Fort Knox, but a few were moved to other locations. Secret locations."

"Cool history lesson, bro," Bones remarked, making no attempt to hide his sarcasm. "What's it got to do with us? If you want us to steal the Declaration for you, I think it's only fair to warn you… There isn't really a treasure map on the back. I checked."

The kidnapper ignored him. "At the end of the war, most of the items were returned to Washington, but not all. With the transition to the Cold War, it was decided that some of these important items should remain where they were. Hidden. And ultimately, forgotten."

"Can we just cut to the chase?" Maddock said. "You want us to find one of these vaults, right? Recover something for you?"

"In a word? Yes."

"Okay. What exactly? And what makes you think Bones and I will be able to find it? You do realize that treasure hunting isn't an exact science. The thing you're looking for may not even exist. The vaults you're talking about… How can you be sure they really exist? They could just be rumors. I don't mind chasing a wild goose now and then, but I can't do the impossible. This is going to take time. A lot of it. Maybe if you let Angel go, we can talk about—"

"The vault exists. I know where it is. And I know what's in it."

"Then what do you need us for?" Bones shot back.

"Another brilliant question. It just so happens that knowing where it is, is not the same as being able to put my hands on it."

Bones nodded incomprehension. "I get it. You want us to steal it for you."

A loud braying sound issued from the phone. "Close, but no cigar. If it was that easy, I wouldn't need you two. No, I'm afraid this task is going to be a little more challenging than that. You see, the item I want you to retrieve isn't some moldy old piece of parchment."

"What then?" Maddock pressed.

"Are you sure you want to know?" There was a strange mewling sound—electronically distorted laughter. "A golden apple."

Bones snorted. "For reals?"

"The apple was a gift—" His intonation changed ever so slightly to emphasize the word "from King Louis XVI of France, given to Benjamin Franklin following the British surrender at the end of the Revolutionary War."

"So not a piece of paper, but a fancy paperweight," Bones sneered. "You're right. That *will* be a little more challenging."

The kidnapper once more ignored his sarcasm. "Are you caught up on your Greek mythology?" He didn't wait for an answer. "Specifically the story of Eris, the goddess of strife... Don't you just love how the Greeks have a god for every little thing?" Another mewl of laughter. "Eris got pissed off because she had been left off the guest list for one of Zeus' swanky soirees. Rather than just crash the party, she decided to stir things up a bit. That was her specialty, after all. She decided to toss a golden apple into the party, an apple inscribed with the words: "To the most beautiful." Now as you can imagine, none of the goddesses were willing to admit that they might *not* be the fairest of them all, and—long story, short—the Trojan War happened. All because of an apple."

"And you think the apple Frenchie gave to Ben is the apple from the myth," Bones said. "Just for the sake of argument, let's say that's true and they are one and the same. Why do you need us to retrieve it for you?"

"The Golden Apple of Discord isn't just a commemorative knick-knack. It is imbued with the power of the goddess of strife. It creates chaos.

"See, I don't think the King meant it as a symbol of congratulations. He knew that the spirit of revolution would soon infect his own kingdom, and so, despite the fact that he supported the colonists during the war, he wanted their experiment in democracy to fail. And what better way to hasten the collapse than toss in a poisoned apple. And it worked. For a while at least, until Franklin got wise and had the apple locked away in a basement somewhere. It stayed there until FDR's archivist brought it out here, and that's where it's been ever since."

"I repeat," Maddock said, forcing the words past grinding teeth. "Why do you need us?"

"The apple was never meant to be hidden away. After seventy-five years, there's no telling how much chaos energy its stored up."

"Chaos energy? What's that even mean?"

"Honestly, I have no idea, but if my suspicions are correct, I'd just as soon not find out the answer first hand."

"So you want us to go in, instead," Bones said. "Take the hit in your place."

"Now you're getting it. The coordinates for the vault's location are in the phone's GPS. Maybe you've already seen it. All you have to do is locate the vault, get inside, and secure the apple. When you have it, I'll contact you with further instructions."

"What if—" But before Maddock could finish the question, the connection was severed and the message "Call ended" flashed on the screen.

Maddock glanced over at Bones. "What do you think?"

Bones gave a rueful smile and shook his head. "A golden apple filled with chaos energy? Sounds pretty hinky to me."

"I have the same feeling. Still, it's not the craziest thing we've gone after. And like it or not, we've got to play along for now. It's the only way to get Angel back." He didn't add that there were no guarantees.

"I guess we better get going then," Bones said, motioning for Maddock to lead the way.

Chapter 6

The cliff didn't turn out as steep as it had initially appeared. Eventually they reached the point to which it had directed them, whereupon the coordinates changed to going 100 meters north.

"What the—?"

"Looks like he's giving us the runaround," Bones observed. "Maybe he's checking to make sure we follow his instructions."

Maddock's sense of dread only deepened, but he didn't give voice to it.

They had to bushwhack through some trees, and the saturated ground threatened to transition into a full-fledged swamp. The coordinates led to another waypoint, just one of several updates to their instructions that seemed intentionally designed to disorient them. After half-an-hour of tromping back and forth, they stopped to grab a drink of water from their canteens.

Bones smacked his lips. "Where does the magic eight ball tell us to go next?"

Maddock pointed to a small rock formation about fifty yards away. The rock seemed to have a blue tint to it.

"That's gneiss."

"Not sure why you think it's nice, Bones."

"Not nice, *gneiss*, the kind of rock."

"Ah. Sometimes I forget you're not as dumb as

you look."

"At least I'm not as dumb as—"

Bones fell silent as a figure appeared next to the rock. Maddock instinctively drew his Walther, then realized who it was, and took off running. "Angel!"

Bones shot out a hand to stop him but his fingers grasped at empty air. With a sigh he pulled out his Glock and started after his friend.

Maddock's pulse was in the stratosphere. Angel waved to him, but he couldn't hear her say anything. He tore through the underbrush, leaving bushes and small trees shattered in his wake.

Then he felt something snag his left ankle. Before he could even think to shake free, he was jerked off his feet. A second later, he was hanging upside down, his foot caught in a thick rope noose, his head five feet off the ground. He had no idea what had happened to his Walther—probably lost somewhere on the forest floor.

His SEAL training kicked in. In an ambush, don't stop and think—react! Maybe this wasn't actually an ambush, but he knew better than to let inertia settle in. He immediately did an inverted crunch and brought his left hand up to grab the rope six inches above his ankle. His right hand uncovered and drew the knife sheathed to his right calf. With a deft motion he sliced the rope between his left hand and his ankle, hanging on tightly as his legs dropped toward the ground and let his shoulder bear the wrenching brunt of the sudden application of gravity. He held on for just a moment, then dropped to the ground in a crouch, knife still in his right hand. He scanned the area and determined two things quickly.

First, Angel was gone.

He'd only seen her for a few seconds, but it was her as clear as day. But he was only twenty yards from the rock formation, and there was no sign of anyone there.

As he spun around, the second problem became apparent and caused him even greater concern.

Bones had vanished as well.

Maddock rushed to the rock formation, which was about ten feet high and maybe fifty feet around. He still didn't see a sign of Angel or Bones. He looked at the GPS. It read *Arrived at Destination*.

Dread crept through his chest. As they had speculated ever since Florida, it was a trap. The kidnappers had wanted them to wind up here. They had also wanted him separated from Bones. But where could Bones possibly be? He wasn't the easiest guy to take down. Maddock would have heard if there were a shot, plus how would they get rid of the body so quickly?

With no answers, Maddock started calling out for Bones and Angel while at the same time searching the area. The forest looked like no one had trodden there recently, but halfway around the rock formation, he found an opening in the stone.

He supposed one might call it a cave, but it was more like a tunnel. Big enough for him to fit into, but not big enough to extend his arms even to the elbows. From the side of the rock, it became nearly vertical within three feet, disappearing into darkness.

He took another look around the area. Aside from this mysterious burrow, it looked like a normal forest. He considered that going blindly into a hole in the ground wasn't the smartest move. Then he recalled that like so much that had happened in the fourteen hours since Angel's kidnapping, he really didn't have any damn choice.

He extracted a headlamp from his pack and secured it on his head, returning his pack to his back. Then with a deep breath he started down into the ground.

His first concern was that he was going to have to use a wedging technique for an unknown period of time to lower himself down the vertical tunnel. As an avid rock climber, this wouldn't be a problem for him, but doing it in the dark was a challenge. And he had no idea if it would widen to the point where he could no longer create the counterforce necessary to continue.

Fortunately, his feet hit some sort of rung about four feet down. As he lowered himself, he found more rungs at eighteen inch intervals. He carefully tested each one before allowing his full weight onto it, but they showed no signs of movement under his weight.

Until both the rung he was holding and the rung on which he was standing disappeared.

Chapter 7

Maddock woke up with a dozen trains chugging through his brain. Not those streamlined passenger trains, but noisy, smoky coal carrying behemoths. He shook his head, but that only made the pain worse. It did clear his mind enough to remember that he had slipped off the ladder rungs.

Scratch that, the rungs vanished.

He didn't remember landing, though. Other images flooded in, mostly buildings engulfed in flames. They weren't things he remembered experiencing, so he figured he must have been dreaming. The dream also contained a voice telling him over and over again to be careful. But careful of what?

Suddenly he sat up, remembering his purpose for coming to Virginia in the first place. He had to find Angel. She had to be here.

He didn't know why he felt so certain about that, but he did. He got to his feet and closed his eyes for a few seconds to stave off a bout of dizziness. When he opened them he felt more solid, and for the first time he looked at his surroundings.

He was in a jungle. Sunlight filtered through a canopy well over a hundred feet above his head, much the way he recalled experiencing certain parts of the Amazon rain forest. The humidity was intense as well, the kind of moist heat only found in the tropics. He stood in the middle of a wide path, the surface of which was a thick bed of a huge variety of castoffs from various flora.

Maddock knew he couldn't be in Virginia any more, and yet he had no sense of any time passing. He rubbed a hand across his chin and felt the same rough five o'clock shadow that had been there when they'd arrived at the trailhead.

Chaos....

The word flashed unbidden through his mind, a fragment of something important hidden in his subconscious, but try as he might, he couldn't bring it to the surface.

He went to look at his watch and realized it was missing. He had dropped the Walther when the rope had jerked him into the air upside down. And his backpack was no longer on his back.

Immediately his hand dropped to his calf, and the presence of his KA-BAR reassured him. His watch and backpack must have been lost during the fall. Then another thought struck him, immediately followed by guilt for it having taken this long.

What happened to Bones?

That thought only lasted a second, as a loud noise hit his ears. It was too high pitched to be a roar, but it carried the same kind of menace. This one was like—

A shuffling noise came from the undergrowth behind him and he whirled. Sprinting toward him was an animal which resembled nothing more than a giant rat. Beyond its size, somewhere between German Shepherd and Great Dane, it had one other feature quite unlike any rat Maddock had ever seen.

It had two massive curved fangs, exactly like pictures of a saber-tooth tiger.

Bones was beyond grumpy when he woke up. He recalled raising his Glock just about the same time Maddock got himself caught in that crazy trap. Then he remembered...

What the hell happened next?

His hand went to his neck and he felt some pain. A quick probing determined that he had some sort of puncture wound. Certainty crept into his consciousness; he had been struck with a tranquilizer dart. Must have been a fast acting one, too, because he could remember falling within a second of the strike. He couldn't remember anything after that until waking up here.

And where is here? It's hotter and wetter than Satan's bidet.

He looked around, taking in the high jungle canopy and the trail on which he lay. These were not the same trees he'd been staring up at just before the dart's tranquilizer did its magic. He got to his feet quickly, shaking off images in his head that must have been from a dream. As an experienced tracker, he recognized a game trail when he saw one. Hanging around was not a great idea.

Bones didn't see many other options, though. He felt certain that Angel had to be somewhere in this place, and the undergrowth was too thick for bushwhacking without some kind of machete. He figured he'd follow the trail for a while and then re-evaluate.

He took inventory and discovered his watch, Glock and backpack missing. He still had his combat knife, which he kept in his left hand. Bones was proficient with either hand, but holding it in his left gave him a slight advantage; most opponents at least subconsciously were more prepared for an attack from the right.

He started down the trail at a steady and nearly silent jog. For the first time since waking, he wondered where Maddock was. Maybe Bones would run into him somewhere in this jungle, but he had to focus on finding Angel first. He knew Maddock would agree.

His mind felt a little bit scrambled as he remembered seeing Angel next to the rock formation. The kidnappers had lured him to this location for some reason, but he had no idea what it was.

Somewhere between fifteen and thirty minutes passed. At first, he just concentrated on moving silently and remaining alert for any sign of Angel or anyone else. But he sensed something wrong. Eventually he figured it out: it was too quiet. A place like this should be vibrating with the sounds of life.

Sometimes creatures will go silent when they

sense a predator, but this didn't feel like that. Bones realized that he had hardly heard a sound since he began jogging. He stopped and listened. He thought he heard a distant sound of running water, but that was it.

Then he finally heard something, a scream cutting through the thick air. It sounded like it was coming from the trail not far in front of him. He took off at a run, suddenly certain that he recognized the source of the scream.

Maddock.

Chapter 8

As the giant rat reached him, Maddock stepped to the side like a matador. One massive fang came within inches of his face, close enough for him to catch a whiff of the creature's foul breath. Then Maddock lashed out at the creature's hindquarters with his knife. It sunk to the hilt and the creature let out a high pitched cry.

Turning, Maddock could see that the massive rodent had stopped nearly on a dime and was lunging again. It looked like a rat, but seemed to have the agility of a cat. He got the knife out in front of him, but couldn't avoid being bowled over by two huge front paws. His entire rib cage and back vibrated from the impact with the ground, and he let out a scream of pain.

He managed a side roll as the fangs dug two deep furrows in the jungle floor. He then swung himself back and leaped onto the rat's neck. The startled creature reared, and Maddock's biceps burned as he held on.

The animal continued thrashing, and Maddock found an opening to drive the knife into one giant eyeball. He heard no cry of pain, but the thrashing stopped and the ground seemed to surge up to meet his skull.

Maddock had to shake off the pain for several seconds after falling, and before he opened his eyes he heard Bones voice call out to him. "Maddock, is everything okay?"

Turning to face his friend, Maddock called out urgently, "Bones, watch out!"

He whirled, expecting an attack at any instant, but saw no sign of the creature. It must have run away, too wounded to continue the battle. Maddock tried to slow his breathing to dissipate the adrenaline of the fight.

Bones had reached him. "Dude, what am I watching out for?"

Maddock stared at him. "Didn't you see that thing? It was huge."

"Didn't I see what? All I saw was you dancing around like a freaking ballerina. A ballerina carrying a knife, but still not all that manly-looking. Don't you think you should concentrated on trying to find my sister?"

Anger coursed through Maddock's veins. He raised his knife. "Screw you, Bones. All I see is you standing around."

Bones' face darkened, and Maddock recognized it as growing rage. He'd seen it a few times, but never been on the receiving end before. That was fine with him, he'd had it with Bones never taking anything seriously.

"Watch out with that knife, little man," Bones growled. "You might cut yourself."

Maddock saw red. Doubts began to rise at the same time, something telling him that this was all wrong. But the anger slammed those thoughts aside. With a roar, Maddock flipped the knife into a backhand grip and lunged in the direction of his best friend.

Chapter 9

Maddock's lunge didn't come close to Bones, who saw it coming and sidestepped with time to spare. Bones swung his own knife toward Maddock, but Maddock had already dropped into a roll and evaded it easily. As Maddock came to his feet, Bones struck again.

Maddock parried the sideways thrust from Bones' knife-wielding left hand, as well as the inevitable cross from the big man's right hand. The two had sparred so many times that neither man had a move which could surprise the other. Maddock allowed the momentum of his left hand to shift after the block and the jab made contact with Bones' chin.

Bones licked his lips but otherwise showed no sign of the impact. He wrapped a huge fist around Maddock's upper left arm and pulled the smaller man closer, attempting to deliver a head butt. Maddock managed to tilt his head just enough that the blow was glancing rather than incapacitating. Then he jammed his knee upwards in a groin strike which elicited a groan and slight bend at the waist from Bones.

As Maddock dropped into a leg sweep, one part of his brain told him that this was not the right move if he wanted to finish his opponent. But another part wanted to see Bones on the ground and vulnerable. The sweep succeeded and Bones went to the ground harder than a smaller man would have.

Maddock sprang to get a knee in the big man's back, but Bones was already rolling as he hit the ground and Maddock's spring ended with his knee in the dirt. The two men both got to their feet quickly and started circling each other, Maddock staying just outside Bones' longer reach.

For just a second, Maddock blinked and questioned the fight. He could have sworn he saw a similar look on his friend's face. But the moment passed and in its place reappeared the overwhelming urge to hurt Bones.

Bones attacked first, a clever feint with both his legs and his right elbow hiding the eventual strike with the knife from the left. Maddock had seen the move before and he met Bones' elbow with a crunching block that caused the knife to soar into the low foliage to the side of the game trail. Rather than press his advantage, Maddock shuffled back, wary of Bones' superior ability in ultra-close quarters.

At least that's what he told himself. Once again, another part of him questioned why he didn't finish it when he had the advantage. Bones must have been thinking the same thing.

"That might have been the last mistake you ever made, micro-man."

Maddock didn't respond, just kept looking for an opening. Sweat was already pouring down his brow and his heart was auditioning for the Olympic hundred meters. Once again, Bones made the first move.

This time, the leg normally used for the feint ended up as the primary weapon. The pain from at least one broken finger created a flash of blindness as Bones' heel launched Maddock's knife out of his hand. Maddock had felt far worse, but this stunned him enough that he stumbled backwards and sank to the ground.

Bones stepped forward, a giant foot serving as an impending wrecking ball. Maddock wasn't sure why Bones paused, but in that instant Maddock no longer felt any anger or desire to inflict harm. As loud as he could manage, Maddock screamed at his friend.

"Bones, what are we doing?"

Angel Bonebrake was pissed. Unfortunately, she had no legitimate targets for her anger. She'd already busted open one heavy bag during her morning's training, something that normally only happened in the last couple weeks before a big fight when she visualized her opponent. Her trainer had merely raised his eyebrows and told her to take the rest of the day off.

Sometime around mid-afternoon, worry started to accompany the anger. At first, she figured that once again Maddock's boat or his crew had taken priority over her. She knew Maddock loved her, but that didn't make it any easier to stomach. But Maddock wasn't answering his phone. Neither was Bones, and neither man was on their boat. *The Sea Foam* remained in its slip, as it had been late last night when Angel went down to investigate.

She had held off contacting any of the crew until the worry set in, not wanting them to think of her as the frail woman needing reassurance. But Maddock had never actually blown off plans entirely. A call to Corey Dean, the crew's techie, confirmed that they all were enjoying some much needed R&R and didn't expect to see Maddock or Bones for over a week.

At five o'clock Angel dialed another number, one she only had in her phone because Maddock had borrowed it on a few occasions. Jimmy Letson answered on the first ring.

"Hi Jimmy, I don't know if you remember me. It's Angel Bonebrake."

"Of course I remember, and it's showing that your phone called mine. I need you to tell me something to verify that it's really you."

"I, um, what are you talking about?"

"I'll tell you once you answer the following questions. In one word, how would you describe your brother?"

Angel chuckled. "Bones is an assclown."

"Right answer. I would also have accepted 'asshat.' Anyway, someone's been spoofing your phone, that's why I asked. For all I know they could be monitoring your phone so we need to keep this short."

"Jimmy, start at the beginning, dammit. What the hell is going on and where are Maddock and my brother?"

Letson gave a brief summary of what had happened with Maddock receiving the texts and the phone spoofing, as well as the claim that Angel had been kidnapped. "I saw the photo attached to the text. It was realistic, no obvious signs of being doctored."

Angel could feel the anger returning. "I wasn't kidnapped! But when I find whoever claimed I was, they're going to wish they'd chosen a different target."

"I don't know who supposedly kidnapped you. But obviously they were trying to lure Maddock and Bones for some reason."

"Sounds like it worked."

"Yeah. I have the exact coordinates where the phone I gave to the guys stopped transmitting. It was in Shenandoah River State Park. I actually got hold of some satellite footage of the area, but the tree cover is too thick to pick anything out."

"Then that's where I'm headed. Is there anything else you can tell me that would help me find them?"

"Well… After the phone went offline I did some more digging. It seems that there have been a few disappearances in that area over the past decade. There's one local sheriff who has done some investigation and even contacted the FBI a couple years back. They told him it was just random disappearances and they couldn't spend any resources on it. Other police in the area figured that was the end of the story, but this guy seems not to believe it. You could give him a shout, see if he has any ideas."

Angel thanked Jimmy and hung up. She packed her bag while her mind raced with all she had learned. A grim smile appeared as she considered someone trying to get one over on Maddock and Bones. Those two had been friends for so long that they didn't even need to communicate to be on the same page. Right now they were probably working together to kick some serious ass.

Chapter 10

Bones' knife stopped less than a centimeter from Maddock's right eye. Maddock blocked the knife-arm, but he didn't follow up with any sort of counter. The two men stared at each other, and then Bones dropped the knife and shook his head.

"You're sometimes a bore Maddock, but I don't think I want to kill you."

Maddock gulped before allowing a small smile. "For a minute there, I wanted you dead. I'm not sure why."

Bones' mouth dropped open. "Maddock, I..."

Maddock took a deep breath. "It's okay, Bones, I don't—"

Bones shook his head. "Nah, I wasn't apologizing. Look at the jungle. I could have sworn it disappeared for a second. Less than a second, just a flicker, really."

Maddock glanced around. "There's something different, some sort of shimmering. But that's got to be a trick of the sunlight. What did you see when things disappeared?"

"Kinda looked like rock walls, but it happened so quick I can't be sure."

"That's weird. Guess we just gotta stay on our toes. So what do we do next?"

"You mean now that I let you live? I'd like to know what made us go after each other. It seemed like the most important thing in the world and now

I can't remember why. Almost like..."

"Like we were drugged." Maddock finished.

"Yeah, that. But then why did it wear off?"

Maddock shrugged. "More questions and no answers. Meanwhile, we have to find Angel. Any sign of her on your end?"

"Nope. After I got hit with a tranquilizer dart, next thing I remember is waking up here and jogging down the trail. What happened to you?"

"I escaped from the trap, found a tunnel, then hit my head falling into it and woke up in the jungle. The giant rat attacked me just before you showed up. In fact..."

He looked around. "I killed it with a knife to the brain. Where did it go?"

Bones frowned. "No sign of a giant rat. Are you sure you didn't dip into the local moonshine? This part of Virginia they make it potent."

"Bones, I don't think we're in Virginia anymore."

"Good point. What did the rat look like?"

Maddock described it, including the huge fangs. Bones nodded. "Sounds like *Sparassodontas*."

"Say what?"

"Extinct carnivore that died out a couple million years ago. They had a pouch like a Kangaroo but otherwise more like a mammal. Basically a rodent version of the saber-tooth tiger. You say you saw one here?"

"Sure seemed like it."

"I wonder if someone's figured out a way to engineer them. That would suck."

"You've got a way with words."

Bones displayed the centermost finger on his left hand.

"And with hand signals."

"My next career will be as an NFL ref."

"Assuming we survive that long. First let's find Angel."

"Goes without saying. I don't think staying on the trail here is a good idea."

"I could get a branch and some vines and rig up my knife like a poor man's machete. That's the only way we'll get anywhere off the trail."

"Works for me. But something's off that I haven't figured out. Why no sounds of life here?"

Maddock cursed to himself. He'd been so focused on finding Angel that he hadn't paid enough attention to his surroundings. That kind of thing could get them killed. "Man, you're right. Strange things are going on."

"Stranger than aliens capturing Noah's Ark?"

Maddock chuckled. "Maybe not that."

"How about stranger than a pack of velociraptors heading for us at full speed?"

"We haven't ever run into velociraptors, Bones."

Bones pointed. "We have now."

Maddock whirled and saw about a dozen creatures, each about ten feet tall sprinting toward them spread out across the trail and its immediate surroundings. They did look like the velociraptors portrayed in the movies, except they had feathers and ran more like giant ostriches.

The two men separated onto different sides of the trail and took out their knives. Hardly another moment went by before three of them targeted Maddock at the same time, giant hooked claws swiping toward his face. Maddock parried one with his knife, slicing off the flesh to which one claw was attached, but he had to drop to his back and roll in order to avoid the other two. As he returned to his feet, animals lunged at him from either side. It only took microseconds, but Maddock's brain had to make a choice he had hoped not to have to make.

Which claw would he avoid and which one would disembowel him?

Chapter 11

Maddock felt his knife enter the midsection of one of the raptors, and braced himself for the blow that was sure to come from the other. Somehow, the second raptor claw only grazed him. Then a solid mound of flesh connected with his shoulder and he flew through the air and landed on his back. His head whiplashed on the ground and the flash of pain triggered stars in his vision.

He shook his head and opened his eyes. Then he closed and opened them again, mouth wide. The raptors were gone.

He got to his feet and looked for Bones. He found him whirling his head from side to side, crouched and ready for an attack.

"Did they run away, Bones?"

Bones slowed his movements but kept scanning the area. "Not exactly. They were taking swings at me one moment, then they just vanished."

"That sounds impossible."

"No crap. But that's what happened. Like Scotty beamed them up or something."

"I don't think they were aliens. What about...this sounds nuts, but maybe they weren't real? Were we hallucinating?"

"You mean like that time I ate the worm at the bottom of the tequila bottle? Possible, but dude, check out your shoulder."

Maddock reached a hand across his shoulder and pulled it away dripping with blood from where the claw had struck him. "Damn. So much for all of this being a hallucination. But we're missing something here."

Chaos energy... Golden apple....

The words flitted through his mind and then were gone just as quickly.

Bones groaned. "I'll tell you what we're not missing. Look at the sky."

Maddock raised his eyes. The sky was cloudless, but a fog had started to descend. It was moving fast, as if propelled by a massive gale. And it was getting closer to ground level. "I've got a bad feeling about this."

"You and me both, bro. Fog doesn't move like that. If that's a natural occurrence, I'm a leprechaun with a huge—"

"I don't think we can outrun it, Bones."

The mist was just reaching the ground, and Maddock coughed once. His head started to swim and he staggered to his knees. As he collapsed to the ground, he heard Bones mumble next to him.

"I'd rather be fighting the raptors."

Chapter 12

"**What brings you** to Warren County?"

Sheriff Brad Danzig's cadence reminded Angel of far western North Carolina where she and Bones had grown up. She knew better than to make the mistake of assuming a slow drawl meant a slow brain. Danzig motioned to her to sit in one of two plush chairs across from the desk in his office. His mustache twitched when he asked the question, and Angel could see curiosity etched in his brown eyes.

"It's about the disappearances."

All levity vanished from Danzig's expression. Angel had decided to just show up rather than call in advance. She'd slept through the red-eye flight and then arrived in Front Royal, Virginia mid-morning. Her only concern was that the sheriff might be out of town, but he had ushered her into his office within minutes after she gave her name to the civilian staffing the front desk.

"What all do you know about them disappearances?"

Danzig hadn't taken a seat. Despite a stature no bigger than Angel's own 5'9", his body now carried a tension which presaged possible violence. Angel took a deep breath.

"I only know that my brother and his best friend have been gone since yesterday morning, and they were last seen in Shenandoah River State Park. Their names are Uriah Bonebrake and Dane

Maddock."

Danzig relaxed, taking several seconds to sit and position himself behind his desk. He leaned back and crossed his hands behind his head.

"Those boys is probably just hiking and having a good old time."

"Maybe. Except I found out that the reason they came here in the first place was that someone convinced them that I had been kidnapped and that they needed to show up if they wanted to see me alive again."

Danzig scoffed. "And how would you know this?"

Angel bit back the urge to say something counter-productive. "My brother and his friend run a marine salvage company. They're former Navy SEALs who also occasionally work with the U.S. Government. Don't ask me exactly what. They're not allowed to tell me about it. I called a guy they sometimes work with... He was tracking their phone and that's how I know where they were last."

She related everything that Letson had told her, but not the computer geek's identity. Danzig's eyebrows crept up a fraction. "This fellow have a name?"

"He does but it's not one I can share with you."

Danzig turned his hands palms-up. "Then I reckon I'm plumb out of time. Once they been gone for forty-eight hours, file a missing persons' report."

"That waiting period isn't mandatory."

"It's how we do things here."

Danzig stood up and extended his hand. Angel didn't move. She met his gaze and stared until he glanced away. Danzig scowled.

"You win the staring contest, Miss Bonebrake. But it's time for you to skedaddle."

"I was told that there have been nearly a dozen disappearances in the past ten years. The FBI doesn't think they are connected. Other law enforcement doesn't think they're connected. But you do. You think they're idiots for ignoring the similarities. I agree with you. If you turn down the opportunity to get more information on another similar disappearance, within twenty-four hours of it occurring, what does that make you?"

Angel's heart raced like it did in the seconds before the bell rang in a fight. She couldn't read Danzig's expression, and she prepared herself for a more forceful removal from the office. Instead, Danzig's face lost its intensity and he slowly lowered himself back into the chair. Angel knew he was thirty-nine years old, but for just a moment he looked eligible for Medicare.

"If I were of a mind to help you, what all do you want?"

Angel slowed her breathing. "I just want to find my brother and my boyfriend."

"They ain't one person are they."

"Of course not." Angel sighed. "One is my fiancée, actually. It's been almost two days since we were supposed to head to the Smokies for some hiking. We were both looking forward to it."

Danzig's tone contained less of a challenge now. "Not meaning any disrespect, but maybe the fellow got some cold feet."

"No way! But even if he did, no way would he just vanish without letting me know." She allowed herself a small smile. "Even if I didn't kill him, my brother would."

"How about that government work you said they did? Think something came up that they ain't allowed to talk about?"

"It's not that kind of work. They're more like free agents, taking jobs when work comes up and they want to do it."

Danzig rubbed three days' worth of stubble on his chin. "I assume that fellow who tracked the phones told you about our disappearances."

Angel nodded.

"He probably also told you that no one but me puts any stock in it being anything other than coincidence."

"That's why I came to see you."

"Thing is, those disappearances is an active investigation. Wouldn't be right of me to share anything with you even if I was inclined."

"But—"

"Before you get all riled up, let me finish. You have the location where those boys were last seen, am I right?"

"Well, at least the last place their phones were active."

"Right, right. Well, ain't nothing stopping the

two of us from heading out there to check it out. This here's a big tourist area, and I got to make shore nothing interferes with that. Can't rightly be having former Navy SEALS go missing on my watch, if you take my meaning."

Angel released a breath she didn't know she'd been holding. She closed her eyes for several seconds to get herself back under control. When she opened them, Danzig was watching her without expression.

"I really appreciate it, Sheriff Danzig. When will you be able to go?"

Danzig stood up and grabbed his hat, gray with a wide brim and gold braid that wouldn't have looked out of place perched atop Robert E. Lee's head. "Ain't no time like the present, Miss Bonebrake."

"You can call me Angel."

He raised his eyebrows. "I don't rightly know if I can do that. Folks might get the wrong idea."

She laughed. "I guess I can see that."

As he moved around the desk toward the door, Angel stood up and put a hand on his shoulder. "Thanks for taking me seriously. Am I wrong or is there something personal for you about these disappearances?"

Danzig's eyes turned hollow at this, and Angel could almost feel the pain reflected in them. When he responded, she had never heard a whisper quite so forceful.

"Nothing was ever more personal."

Chapter 13

"**Bones, are you** dead?"

Maddock kneeled alongside his supine friend, shaking him by the shoulder. He remembered them both succumbing to the descending mist, then nothing until waking up thirty seconds ago with a headache and a dry mouth. Normally that state only followed a prolonged encounter with a good tequila.

Bones wasn't moving yet, and he shook the big man again. A giant fist sprang up and grabbed him by the neck.

As Maddock reached to wrest free of his friend's grasp, Bones' eyes opened.

"Anyone ever tell you that your breath stinks?"

Escaping from Bones' grip, Maddock allowed himself a chuckle. "Your sister doesn't seem to mind."

"She's always had crappy taste." Bones got to his feet and looked around. "Where are we?"

Instead of the jungle, they were now in a mountainous area much more like Virginia. They had woken in a tiny patch of rock and grass with a view of a forest gradually sloping away from them and modest mountains rising beyond that. Behind them, the forest was thicker and strewn with rocks in a manner typical of the eastern U.S.

Maddock put his hands on his hips. "Maybe Virginia, but I don't think we should assume anything. The air is pretty crisp, so we're probably higher than we were when we parked."

Bones scanned the horizon. "Am I the only one thinking Angel's not around here?"

Maddock clenched his fists. "Nope. Which means we have to get out of here and get back to some sort of civilization. That means either finding a stream and following it downhill or heading for the highest ground in the area and trying to figure out where we are."

"That's easy. We head for high ground but if we come across a stream, we follow that instead. Looks to me like that peak there is only about three miles away."

Maddock nodded and they started hiking. His dry mouth had disappeared but he was concerned that if they were out here long enough the lack of food and water would become a problem. He didn't know how long they had been unconscious—either time in fact—but he wasn't hungry yet.

After an hour, they had reached the top of the peak. They had seen no sign at all of water. Unfortunately, their effort hadn't gained them anything. Bones stood smashing one fist into the other palm as they gazed out over the forest.

"It's like that movie Groundhog Day. This looks almost exactly like the terrain we saw when we first woke up."

Maddock was about to answer when the sound of a rifle shot echoed from the forest in front of them. At almost the same instant, they heard what had to be the shot striking a tree ten feet from where they stood.

Neither man hesitated in sprinting toward the nearest sizable rock formation, fifty yards away and perpendicular to where Maddock figured the shot had originated. Before they had made it halfway, another shot tore into the ground three yards in front of them.

"Don't stop, Bones!"

"Goes without saying."

Another shot chipped the rocks three seconds before they arrived, but they managed to get safely to their destination. The formation was moss-covered and about eight feet tall and four feet wide. Several thick clumps of spruce trees ringed the area, providing as much cover as they were bound to find.

"Who the hell is shooting at us Bones?"

Bones shook his head. "With everything else that's happened, I think the real question is why it took this long for someone to shoot at us."

Another bullet took a gouge out of the closest tree. Bones looked at the splintered hole. "Oh, crap."

Maddock followed his glance and picked up on the source of Bones concern. The round had struck only four feet off the ground. It came from a different direction than the other shots. And no one could have covered the ground that quickly from the origin of the first shots to the new location. "Two shooters."

"Or more." Bones swore. "This is BS. That last one was from really close by."

He grinned a grin worthy of Satan himself. "Time to do the last thing they expect."

"Wait, Bones, don't—" The words died in Maddock's throat. Bones had launched himself in the direction from which the shot had come.

Maddock had been angry almost beyond words when he saw the initial text from the kidnappers. When Bones had attacked him earlier, the rage he felt for a short time was nearly as great. Now, not only was his fiancée kidnapped, his best friend was running straight into the path of a gunman. His frustration exploded into an incandescent roar and he launched himself after Bones.

And tripped over his own feet as the forest floor disappeared before his very eyes.

Chapter 14

Baltimore, MD

Richard Cranmore was running. He didn't know exactly why. He didn't even know where. He just knew that something compelled him to keep going.

Cranmore was a large man, with at least a case of Milwaukee's finest covering the tiny six pack which had formerly constituted his abs. He hadn't run in at least twenty years. As such, it didn't take long for his body to override the compulsion to keep going. His stop was abrupt, and his vision dimmed as he doubled over trying to achieve five times his normal oxygen intake.

About the time his breathing slowed from a jet engine to an underpowered import, he became aware of his surroundings. He was only two blocks away from his workplace. His relief at this recognition was short-lived when he became aware of what he held in his hands.

A large bag of cash.

Many people would be quite pleased to find themselves with a stash of hundreds, but Cranmore was not among them. He worked as a bank teller. Two blocks away. He took another deep breath as his brain struggled to remember what had happened.

Then he heard the sirens.

To his credit, Cranmore started moving immediately. Despite having no idea how he wound up with all this cash, he knew it must have come from the bank. He had to get back there. Fleeing would just make things worse. He couldn't manage more than a brisk walk, but he soon was opening the door to the main branch of the Baltimore Credit Union.

His entry into the lobby froze everyone inside. He couldn't see any customers, but more security guards than normal were there. It seemed that the entire staff was gathered in the lobby.

The inaction didn't last long. Within seconds, one guard had snatched the bag out of his hand. Another had grabbed his hands and cuffed them behind his back with enough force that he screamed in pain at the torque on his shoulder.

The branch manager, Joseph Perez, stood a few feet in front of him scowling. Perez addressed the guard holding Cranmore's cuffs. "Bring him into my office."

As they made their way up the stairs to the executive offices, Cranmore's stomach did a couple of flips. He still couldn't remember how he wound up blocks away with all that money, but the reaction of his co-workers suggested that whatever had happened was far from kosher.

After Cranmore and the guard entered the office, Perez slammed the door behind them. His dark features formed a deep scowl. "What in the name of God were you doing?"

All at once a memory came back to Cranmore. He swallowed hard before answering his boss. "You pulled me from my window and said you needed help in the vault. We went in, you handed me the bag, and told me to meet you outside. I thought it was strange, but for some reason I did what you said. Then, as I was leaving, I heard people yelling at me, saw the guard draw his gun, and I ran. Next thing I knew, I was around the corner and had… temporary amnesia, I guess. Then I came back to find you."

Perez nearly had smoke erupting from his ears. "That's the most ridiculous story I've ever heard."

Cranmore felt his face getting hot. "But it's true, I swear!"

Perez stared at him for a long second, then shook his head. "Fine, if you want to stick to this fantasy, there's an easy way to deal with it."

He looked at the guard. "Let's go to the security booth."

The security booth was located on the first floor behind a door which required a retinal scan by the guard. Cranmore could feel dozens of eyes on him walking back down the stairs and waiting for the guard to complete the authentication. He didn't notice any police yet, but he could hear the sirens close by.

Once inside the security booth, the guard called up the relevant video camera footage. Cranmore saw himself behind his teller window, handling a transaction for a man dressed in a bowler hat and an Oxford shirt. Several times while waiting for Cranmore to finish, the man took a drag on an e-cigarette. Then the man gave a flick of the e-cig and for just a second, a cloud of gray mist engulfed the teller.

The man began spinning the e-cig like a baton and speaking rapidly, though the surveillance footage did not pick up the words. The mist dissipated within seconds, and Cranmore saw himself pause and then hurry away from his station and out of range of the camera.

Perez looked sharply at him. "Why did you leave?"

Cranmore stammered. "I-I-I don't know."

Less than a minute later the video showed Cranmore returning, this time at a run and carrying the bag of cash. After watching himself sprint out the front door of the bank, Cranmore put his head in his hands.

"Care to change your story about me ordering you to do it?"

Cranmore looked up. "It must have been that customer, whatever he sprayed from that e-cigarette hypnotized me!"

Perez scoffed. "That's even dumber than blaming it on me."

"But you all saw the mist! Those things aren't supposed to do that." Cranmore protested.

Perez shook his head. "Tell it to the jury."

A knock sounded on the door, and they all glanced at the monitor which showed the outside of it. Perez nodded to the guard, who opened the door and let in the assistant manager along with a uniformed police officer. The assistant manager carried the bag that Cranmore had stolen.

"What's the problem?"

The assistant manager held up the bag. "Officer Rivers here asked me if all the money was still in the bag. With the shock of Rick coming back, we hadn't counted it yet. But when I did, I—" He cast a sad glance in Cranmore's direction.

"Out with it." Perez snapped.

The assistant manager took a deep breath.

"Half of the money is gone."

Chapter 15

Maddock stumbled when the forest floor disappeared. He didn't go all the way down, though. He stopped himself and then stood stock still, taking in the new scene. Instead of seeing cool, crisp mountain air and a vast forest, he was inside a large cavern at least a hundred yards in diameter, with the top more than forty feet over his head. It was dim, but not dark, as lights were visible throughout the area.

Bones was sitting about twenty feet away, whirling his head from side to side with wild urgency. The big man was clutching one hand to his right shoulder. Maddock called out to him.

"You okay, Bones?"

Bones stopped moving and looked at Maddock. "If by okay, you mean caught in the Twilight Zone with Rod Serling yanking our chains then, yeah, I'm okay."

"So you're seeing the cave, too?"

Bones nodded. "We've seen some weird crap, but this could be the weirdest. A mountain landscape one instant, a dungeon the next."

Maddock's brain had started to race. "It was all an illusion or a hologram. The jungle, the mountains, the creatures."

"Yeah, but those things made physical contact with us. You were even wounded."

Maddock slid his left hand over to the wound

on his right shoulder. As he felt the area, he let out a whistle. "This feels more like abrasion from contact with the ground than it does a claw wound. In fact, I remember thinking there's no way that raptor could have missed tearing out my guts."

Bones furrowed his brow. "I bet those asshats drugged us. Otherwise we would have noticed that we were striking air when we swung at them."

"That's probably what the mist was. I remember—" He stopped.

"What?"

"That's odd, I can't remember the creatures I was fighting when you found me."

"Are you going senile on me? They were, um... Oh hell no, I can't remember either."

"Drugs might explain that, too, though it's kinda scary. They would also explain us trying to kill each other for no reason."

Bones smirked. "No reason? Come on, you know better than to lob me a softball like that."

"I kinda figured we had enough on our minds, what with being trapped in a giant cave with no food or water and no idea where we are."

"That's the perfect time to give you crap."

"I stand corrected. I think we need to try to figure out how to get out of here, though. Let's work our way around the walls in different directions, see what we can find."

Bones didn't answer, he just followed Maddock across the cavern until they reached the nearest wall. The light they had glimpsed from a distance came from torches which were mounted in sconces every twenty feet or so. They protruded from the wall almost ten feet off the cavern floor, well out of even Bones' reach.

The humidity had returned to levels Maddock associated with northern Virginia, but the temperature was lower than it normally was there in the summer. That could be explained by the cavern, but Maddock wasn't at all confident that they were still in Virginia. Or even in a cavern for that matter.

"We had to get in here somehow, so that means we can find the way out. I'll go clockwise."

"Why do you get the fun direction?"

Maddock didn't bother responding, he just started walking. He moved steadily but without rushing, running his hands along the wall and devoting all his senses to identifying anything unusual.

All too soon, he and Bones met halfway around from where they had started. "Any luck?"

He shook his head "You?"

"Not a damn thing. I suppose the way out could be higher up the walls or in the ceiling, but that would mean they had to lower some kind of rope or ladder. Possible, but we'll never find anything that high."

"Leaving us with the ground. Which means—man, I'm not gonna like what we have to do next."

"Yep. We have to search in a grid pattern, just like hunting for buried treasure..." He trailed off as the words brought him close to a memory.

Treasure... We were supposed to find something. Something made of gold....

"It's a lot more fun looking for buried treasure."

Maddock gave up trying to retrieve the memory. "Come on, Bones, you always hate methodical searches. It doesn't matter what we're looking for."

"Shut up, Maddock."

After agreeing on a division of labor, they began methodically walking back and forth across the bottom of the cavern. Maddock had to take it slowly, as the lights on the walls cast shadows that made picking out details on the floor more difficult. Nothing like having to examine every square inch of a place to make you appreciate how much surface area it contained.

With no watch Maddock couldn't be sure how much time had passed, but he figured it was over an hour before a shout came from Bones.

"I am the *Man*!"

Maddock rushed to his friend's side, at a spot close to the dead center of the cavern. "What'd you find?"

Bones pointed to the floor. "A pretty weak attempt to hide some hinges."

Maddock knelt on the floor and saw what appeared to be rubber flaps painted the same color as the cavern. Underneath them were indeed hinges. They contained some rust, but didn't seem to be deteriorated much. The hinges were held in place by what looked like two giant rivets or bolt heads in each one. He ran his hands along the floor next to them.

"Feels like ...yeah, some sort of seam here. There's a whole section that's rubber, with another flap right here."

He pulled on another section of floor, and exposed a rusted metal handle recessed into what was clearly some sort of portal. A tug on the handle yielded no movement.

Bones nudged him aside. "Allow me."

Bones jerked the handle up, but again created no movement. He tried again with more effort, but the result was the same. "I'm thinking this one will be brains over brawn."

Maddock stroked his stubble. "It probably locks from the inside. If pulling the handle isn't doing it, then we have to go after the hinges. Maybe find some rocks we can smash them with?"

"I found just the thing during that boring grid search." Bones jogged away and returned a few seconds later carrying two pieces of sandstone, each just small enough to be held in one hand. "These should be solid enough to take a bit of punishment. Not as hard as iron but it's the best we can do. There's more of them after we break these."

He offered one to Maddock before kneeling by the hinges. He looked up. "Time to destroy things."

Bones lowered the rock, and a loud crack echoed through the cavern. He repeated the motion and soon got into a rhythm. After about three minutes, his rock had crumbled to the point where it was no longer accomplishing anything.

"Your turn, slacker. I'll go get more."

As Bones trotted off, Maddock started hammering with his rock. He could see some chips in the hinge Bones had attacked, but nothing that seemed close to getting it loose. He resigned himself to it taking a while.

Three times Bones returned with more rocks and they took turns pounding. Maddock could see progress now, with half of the first hinge missing. His shoulder ached some, but a lifetime of physical training had prepared him for a lot worse than this. As Bones jogged off yet again, he set about his task.

A few moments later, he noticed the mist again.

The effect was different in the cavern than it had been when they thought they were in more open spaces. But he had no doubt about its purpose. "Bones, get your ass back here. We have a big problem."

While Bones was running, Maddock started hammering like a madman with the rock. The first hinge gave way just as Bones arrived. Maddock tore what remained of it out of the ground and then grabbed the handle again. This time there was some give in the area formerly occupied by the hinge, but they still weren't close to getting the whole portal loose.

Bones dropped to his knees as the mist descended to within ten feet of them. He snatched the broken hinge and began using it to pound the other one.

The harder metal did damage faster than the stones had, but Maddock started coughing when the mist reached head level. He dropped to his knees. "Anything I can do, Bones?"

Bones didn't stop his frenzied pummeling.

"Pray."

Chapter 16

Steve Renfield adjusted his tie before he activated
the video conference. Not that his appearance
mattered to anyone, but he wanted to delay giving
the bad news for a few more seconds. With a sigh he
pressed an area on the sixty-inch touch screen in
front of him, revealing the face of Alex Scano on the
other end of the conference.

"Mr. Scano, we have a big problem"

The face on the other end was intense, and
Renfield could make out the ugly scar on the man's
throat. He had survived both a fatal plague and a
knife across his throat, and people whispered that
Scano was invincible. On the video call, Scano's lack
of reaction was scarier than a display of anger would
have been.

"How many times have I told you to call me
Alex? What's the problem?" His voice contained a
permanent rasp, the result of the throat wound.

"The second dose apparently didn't take.
Maddock and Bonebrake found the door."

Scano's lips twitched. "How exactly did they do
that?"

"They were, um, conducting a grid search."

"And you didn't notice them doing this?"

"Well, ah, you see they didn't...I mean they..."
Renfield's voice trailed off.

Scano growled. "We all know it's not perfected
yet. That's why we're testing it. That's why your

team is right there on site monitoring them."

"Yes, sir, um, Alex. The real world test was successful, though."

Scano emphasized every other word in his next sentence. "I know the real world test was successful, you moron. Don't change the subject. Can I at least assume you drugged them again?"

Renfield swallowed. "Of course. We started that thirty seconds before I called."

"Which means they might not be out yet. At least the porthole is secured from the inside."

Renfield didn't answer right away, and Scano pounced. "There's something you're not telling me."

"I was getting to it. We noticed that the dose had worn off when we discovered them pounding the porthole with rocks. We're, um, not sure how close they came to getting through."

Scano's voice lowered an octave. "We will discuss your future at ScanoGen very soon. In the meantime, make sure the situation is taken care of."

"Yes, um, Alex. Ah, what do you want us to do with them?"

"Knock them out for at least twelve hours to allow time to ship them here. We need to keep them alive long enough to study their brains and figure out what happened. You think you can handle the simple matter of transporting men who are already unconscious?"

"Yes, sir."

"The next time I want to hear from you is with the news that they are in transit."

Scano's hand moved toward the screen and then it went dark on Renfield's end. He shook his head and spoke to himself. "That went well."

Moving just a few feet, he stood behind one of the other members of his security team who was monitoring the camera covering Maddock and Bonebrake. The mist had descended to the point where he could hardly make out the shapes of his two captives. He put a hand on the security man's shoulder.

"Vitals?"

"They're not unconscious yet. Should be very soon, though."

A raised voice carried from another workstation in the control room. "Sir, you better take a look at this."

Renfield moved quickly and found himself looking at another monitor. This one showed the rock formation in Shenandoah River State Park, the one through which Maddock and Bonebrake had initially entered the facility. Two figures could be seen approaching in the distance.

"Is that...?"

"Looks like our favorite sheriff."

"Just great. I thought for sure we had him beaten in the last election."

"Never bet on politics. I don't recognize the other person yet."

Renfield stared at the screen for a moment before the identity of the other figure hit him. He felt acid beginning the trek from his stomach to his esophagus. It wasn't bad enough that Maddock and Bonebrake had come within a whisper of escaping, or that the nosy sheriff was too close for comfort. Now they had to contend with another person he'd hoped would never get within a country mile of ScanoGen.

The other figure on the screen was Angelica Bonebrake.

Chapter 17

Angel and Sheriff Danzig approached the rock formation. She looked down at the GPS app on her phone and stopped in her tracks.

"We're here, Sheriff."

Danzig nodded. "Yep. This here spot seen a couple other disappearances too."

Angel turned her head sharply. "Wait. You knew about this spot? Why didn't you tell me?"

Danzig touched the brim of his hat. "Miss Bonebrake, you're a civilian. There's a lot of things I know about this case that I haven't shared with you."

Danzig ended discussion by scanning the forest floor between them and the rock. He pointed an index finger crooked enough that it must have been broken more than once in the past. "Looks to be a right struggle happened there."

Angel nodded. "You're right. I see signs of two people walking side by side right before there. One of them had huge feet, just like my brother."

Danzig regarded her with signs of interest. "That there is some fine tracking skills."

Angel smiled. "From the time we could walk, our grandfather taught me and Bones about tracking and moving in the woods. This is like a neon sign compared to tracking a deer over ten miles of rolling forest."

Danzig's chuckle was a rasp. "I reckon it is. You

being a civilian and all, I guess I should have asked if you was armed?"

"If I say yes, are you going to confiscate it?"

"No. Just wanting the lay of the land."

"I'm not that big into guns, but I do have a knife. You need to see it?"

"Nah. How well can you use it?"

Angel grinned. "Better than I can track. Speaking of which, let's see where they went after the struggle."

When they arrived at the rock formation itself, Angel shook her head. "I'm thinking it was at least three and maybe four people. They came from at least two different directions. Two of them were carrying something really heavy the last thirty yards."

Danzig chewed his bottom lip. "Where did they go from here?"

They circled the rock formation, finding no sign of tracks leading away. Angel smashed the heel of her hand against the rock. "Damn it, I know they were here. And they didn't just fly away."

Danzig spoke almost under his breath. "They surely did not. I been to this spot ten times and ain't found a damn thing. But we'll look anyway. Search every inch of this here rock."

Angel put her hands on her hips and her lips trembled. "And if we don't find anything?"

"Then we look again."

Maddock gasped, whether from the mist or the six-foot fall onto his shoulder he couldn't say. He reached back up through the portal and dragged Bones down into the hallway with him. Bones had succumbed to unconsciousness just as he had broken through the second hinge, his exertions undoubtedly causing his heart to pump the toxic air through his lungs more quickly.

Maddock laid him on his side and started firm raps on his upper back. Bones had only been out for a few seconds, and it only took a few more before he started coughing. Maddock stepped away to give him space.

When Bones got to his feet, he smashed his head into the ceiling and said a word unequivocally not allowed on network television. Maddock bit back a smile.

"You okay, Bones? I owe you one for getting that door open."

Bones coughed again. "You owe me so many I lost track. You had a chance to scope out this place?"

"Nope, we just got here."

They were in a long hallway with walls, floor and ceiling constructed of smooth concrete. The ceilings were right at six feet high and florescent tubes provided minimal illumination every ten feet along the top of the walls.

Bones bumped his head as he turned to look the other way down the hallway. "It's a damn bunker. Not even any graffiti."

Maddock said, "Well, there are only two directions we can go. Any ideas?"

Bones fixed his gaze on the floor, his eyes methodically scanning. Then he pointed to their left. "This way. More signs of traffic that way."

Maddock shook his head. It all looked hard and gray to him, but if Bones said there were signs then there were. They began to walk, and Maddock took out his knife.

Bones reached down and did the same, chuckling as he came up. "I must still be a little out of it, not thinking to have Mr. KA-BAR ready."

Maddock said nothing, but his mind was on what they might find at the end of the hallway. He didn't expect to make it out without a fight. He knew that Bones would have figured out the same thing. He allowed all five of his senses to focus and maximize his chances of reacting quickly to the unexpected.

The locked door was not really a surprise. They'd been walking for about ten minutes when the hallway turned and they came to a steel door with a keypad on it. Both men quickly lunged back around the corner as soon as they saw it.

Maddock spoke not much above a whisper, "Something tells me our quiet walk is about to get loud."

"No doubt. It'd be even worse if I had explosives. Maybe I should try to kick the door down."

Maddock frowned. "I don't know. If it didn't work, they would know we're here."

"There was a security camera above the door so they probably know already."

"Then we better move quickly. Did you see what was above the security camera?"

Bones groaned. "I knew you were going to suggest it. Yeah, I saw the ventilation grate. We're not all puny like you and can fit into spaces like that."

"Tell you what, Bones. You try smashing the door and I'll try the ventilation shaft. Whoever gets killed first loses."

"What if it's a tie?," Bones growled. "Fine, but I get to go first. No way I'm gonna be staring at your butt the whole time."

Maddock motioned with one palm toward the corner. Bones took a deep breath and moved quickly back that direction, Maddock right on his heels.

At the door, Bones reached up to the grate and gave it a tug. It moved a little bit, but didn't come down. Bones tried again, this time with both hands, and the grate tore off its hinges and nearly struck Maddock in the face.

"Careful, man."

"Sorry, I forgot how strong I am."

Fortunately the opening was wider than his shoulders, so Bones stuck his arms through and pulled himself up high enough that he could see into the horizontal shaft. After a second, he dropped back down.

"Well, it's not the smallest I've ever seen."

Maddock couldn't resist. "That's what she said."

Bones grinned. "Hey, there's hope for you. The shaft is concrete, so it should support our weight. Here goes nothing."

First his upper body disappeared into the opening, then his legs as well. Maddock followed him. Maddock could move okay and he didn't suffer from claustrophobia, but all things considered he would have preferred to be almost anywhere else.

Within seconds they were over whatever space was behind the door. After travelling about twenty feet, Bones stopped and squeezed his head partially around toward Maddock. "Another grate."

"Can you see anything through it?"

"Yeah. A room with some monitors and at least three people in it. There must be steps down behind the door, because it's at least a ten foot drop to the floor."

"Could we drop right onto a couple of the people?"

"That's a negative. We're in the middle of the room and they're against a wall. No idea if there are others I can't see either."

Maddock thought for a moment.

"If you can get over the grate, I say we keep going. Maybe get past here and drop down into an unoccupied room."

"You're assuming they won't hear us."

"Well they haven't so far. If they had, they--"

Bullets suddenly tore through the ceiling right behind Maddock. Bones gave a roar and smashed his fist through the grate, then dove headfirst through the opening. Maddock was right behind him, though his smaller size allowed him to squeeze his body through feet first. He just hoped Bones had managed to hit the floor in a controlled roll rather than cracking his head open.

Another roar from the big man confirmed that he had landed safely. Before he had even landed, Maddock had identified both the man with the gun aimed at the ceiling and the nearest other target.

Bones was already moving in the direction of the gunman so Maddock allowed his knees to bend when he landed and then quickly sprang toward the second man, who was trying to clear a pistol from a holster.

The move for the pistol died as Maddock smashed the hilt of his knife against the man's temple. It was a risk not to simply slice the man's throat, but Maddock wasn't going to kill any more people than he had to. Maddock grabbed the gun, a Glock not unlike the one Bones carried. He didn't stop moving though, diving in a different direction into a roll and scanning for threats as he came out of it.

Bones was grappling with the first gunman, whose compact automatic rifle pointed straight in the air. Actually, grappling overstated the amount of resistance the man was able to muster against

Bones. In another second Bones had the man in a chokehold with one arm, the gun in his other hand.

Maddock saw three other people in the room. Two were seated, clear expressions of terror on their faces. The third stood near the five steps that led up to the door. The third man was bringing a pistol to bear on Bones.

Almost without conscious decision, Maddock fired two shots from the Glock. The first knocked the pistol out of the man's hand and the second created a neat hole in the center of the man's forehead. The power in the shot knocked the corpse back onto the steps.

Maddock swung his gun toward the two remaining men. "Hands in the air!"

Their hands couldn't have moved more quickly if they were connected to the power grid. Out of the corner of his eye, Maddock saw Bones lower the now unconscious gunman to the ground. Bones said, "He'll be taking a nap now."

Maddock nodded, taking deep breaths to slow his heart rate. He maintained a watch on the two seated men, though they looked too scared to even blink. "One of you guys want to tell me what the hell this place is?"

Before they could answer, Bones' voice sounded. He had walked over to the dead man on the stairs. "Nice shooting, Maddock. I told you the Glock is the better gun."

"I guess they're okay in a pinch."

Bones looked down at the body "You gave this

one a third eye." Then he looked back at Maddock with a twisted smile. "Very Zen."

Chapter 18

"**Start talking.**"

Bones towered above the only two men who remained both alive and conscious. Unlike the other three, these men were unarmed and cowering in their seats. One had his hair tied up in a man-bun and the other had the requisite freckles to accompany his red hair. Both faces were chubby enough to suggest they were unaccustomed to any kind of physical effort.

The redhead answered first. "Um, um, we just work here!"

Bones flicked his palm at the back of the speaker's head. "He did NOT say 'just following orders,' did he Maddock?"

Maddock shrugged. "Sounded like it to me."

Bones cracked his knuckles with a glint in his eyes directed at the man. "You want to try again, or do I get to have some fun?"

The redhead swallowed. "Okay, okay. Just don't hit me again."

"That was a love-tap. If I'd hit you, you'd be unconscious like your friends. Final chance. What is this place?"

"It's our lab. We're scientists and this is where we run clinical trials for our new drug."

"If you're running clinical trials, where are your subjects?"

The redhead looked around with nervous eyes,

then settled them on Maddock. "Well...you are."

Maddock clenched his fists. "So all this was a medical experiment?"

Both men nodded and Man-bun spoke eagerly. "That's right!"

"What kind of medical experiment has its researchers kidnap their test subjects?"

Man-bun blinked and looked at his colleague for help. When none was forthcoming, he adopted an expression of surprise. "Kidnapped? I had no idea—"

Bones backhanded him in the face. "That's bullcrap."

Redhead started to blubber, tears dripping out of his eyes. Bones shook his head. "Pathetic."

Man-bun slumped down in his seat. "What do you want from us? Okay, of course we knew the subjects weren't doing this willingly. And we never asked what happened to them afterwards. The guys with the guns didn't seem too keen on questions. Neither did Mr. Scano."

Maddock's ears perked up. "Alex Scano? He's dead."

Man-bun shook his head. "He just talked to us earlier today."

Bones said. "Like a bad penny, Maddock."

Maddock considered this development, and as he did, a few fragments of memory bubbled to the surface.

Angel had been kidnapped... Or had she? It didn't matter. It had all been part of an elaborate ruse to draw him and Bones into Scano's web. Now he remembered something else. An electronically distorted voice telling him to find... Something about chaos or discord... A golden apple... No, *the* Golden Apple that had once belonged to the goddess Eris....

It didn't matter. That had all been part of the ruse... An idea planted like a post-hypnotic suggestion, designed to make them more receptive to the crazy hallucinations caused by Scano's drug.

He took a step forward and both scientists flinched. "Let's get back on track here. What does this new drug do? If Scano's involved, it must either kill billions of people or control them."

Man-bun gulped again. "Well, you could certainly use it to control people. B-but that's not what Mr. Scano said. This is going to be used to help mentally ill people."

"How exactly does putting two former soldiers in a cave with hologram animals test a drug designed for that?"

"They weren't holograms. All of that was in your minds."

Bones blinked. "No way. We both saw exactly the same crap."

Now that he was talking about science, man-bun no longer sounded terrified. "That's because the drug works along with virtual reality technology. It's kind of like the old subliminal messages except a thousand times more effective. Something about how the drug targets the part of the brain that connects to the optic nerves."

"And ScanoGen developed this drug? What's it called?"

"It's called *Brainwash*. Actually, the drug occurs naturally in a plant that grows only in a remote region in Africa. It's actually found in the spores of a fungus that grows on the plant, but nowhere else. It is extremely difficult to reproduce. Without the VR, it's just like a weaker version of peyote. The VR is what we developed."

This time Maddock was the one delivering the slap, terminating the smug expression on man-bun's face. Bones gave a golf clap.

"Nice, Maddock, but you need to put more wrist into it."

Maddock lowered his face closer to man-bun. "The name of the drug says it all. It's hard to believe you're stupid enough to believe that something like this will be used to help people. But maybe you are. In which case I know you're not in charge at this facility. Who is?"

Man-bun pointed to the man whom Bones had choked into submission. Maddock and Bones had found duct tape in a cabinet in the room and bound the hands, wrists and ankles of the two incapacitated gunman.

Maddock gestured to Bones. "I think naptime is over."

Bones went over to the supine figure and

jerked him up by the front of his shirt. The man's eyes were closed and his head lolled forward. Bones put his mouth close to the guy's ear and started doing an abysmal imitation of the trumpet notes in Reveille. The volume of his warbling probably could have woken the gunman Maddock had shot in the head.

The man's head jerked up and his eyes opened in panic. He twisted his head to the side and the first thing he saw was Bones' angry face. Maddock watched him take a couple of seconds to figure out what had happened. A look of calculation appeared, which Maddock wanted to eliminate as quickly as possible.

"Bones, don't you think this guy would be more comfortable on the floor with your knee in his back?"

"I know my knee would be more comfortable."

Bones tossed the man on the floor and dropped to a knee. He turned the man's head sideways and pinned it in place with one huge paw.

"We'll start with an easy one. What's your name?"

Maddock interjected. "Before you think about lying, consider that I'm watching your buddies over here and I have a feeling they won't be able to avoid giving it away if you lie."

The man on the ground grumbled. "Steve Renfield."

Maddock said, "Good. We really only have two more questions."

Bones looked at Maddock. "We do?"

"Well maybe three. First question is, where is Angel Bonebrake?"

"I'm having trouble talking with my face squashed into the floor."

Maddock snarled. "Deal with it. I'm having trouble coming up with a reason not to pull the trigger on your partner's gun."

Renfield gritted his teeth. "Fine. We didn't touch your precious girlfriend."

Bones increased the pressure in the hand on Renfield's neck. "You're talking about my sister too, jerkoff."

"Right, right. All we did was spoof her phone and get creative with Photoshop. I swear we never laid a hand on her."

Renfield's words carried the ring of truth. Maddock felt a lump forming in his throat as he realized that Angel had most likely been safe this whole time. He ruthlessly forced those feelings aside. "For your sake we better never find out any different. Next question is how do we get out of here?"

"You can get out the same way you came in. That door over next to the stairs opens to the ladder that goes up to the park."

Maddock saw something in Renfield's eyes. "How long is the climb?"

"About two hundred feet."

"You expect us to believe that you guys come to work every day by hiking to a stone formation, opening a secret door, and descending a ladder in a tunnel barely big enough to fit a single person? Try again. Quickly."

"Okay, okay." Renfield protested. "Walk around behind the monitors and the door is there. There are half a dozen golf carts and you drive about five miles before you get to an elevator which takes you up to the surface."

"That sounds more like it. Are we going to come out facing a bunch of guys with guns?"

"Just a single guy behind a desk. Um, he does have a gun, though."

Bones looked at Maddock. "We can handle that."

Maddock nodded. "Yes we can. Okay, you're doing well. Here's the final question. Where can I find Alex Scano?"

Renfield furiously tried to move his head, but Bones held firm. Finally he stopped struggling. "If he finds out I told you, he won't just kill me, he'll kill my family."

Maddock felt a small twinge of compassion, but he didn't have much difficulty pushing it aside when he recalled Renfield aiming a gun at them just a few minutes earlier. "I really don't care. Bones, do you care?"

"I've never given less of a crap."

"Right. So, Renfield, I guess I need to admit something to you. We don't really like to kill people. Especially not Bones. Bones much prefers torture. In fact, the Cherokees were well-known for the creative ways they inflicted suffering."

Maddock knew this was not entirely true, but he figured Renfield would have heard of scalping at least. Bones was nodding his head.

"This is true. In fact, I'm not sure I want you to talk right away. There's something I've been wanting to try for a while now. Maddock, we'll need to expose some of the wires in that outlet over there. Renfield, did you know that it's possible to complete an electrical circuit through the human body? Sure you do. You work with scientists. Well, I've got an idea for an experiment. I'll put the positive wire goes in one of your nostrils. The negative wire goes right on the tip of your—"

"You guys aren't going to give up, are you?"

Maddock bent down and looked him in the eye. "I'm sure you were given information about our backgrounds. I doubt there was a single word in there about us ever giving up."

"Fine. You win. Scano spends most of his time at the building in—"

"Hey Maddock, you gotta look at this right now." Bones interjected. He was still holding Renfield down, but his attention had shifted fully to a video monitor off to their left.

Maddock followed Bones' gaze. He did a double-take, not believing his eyes. Then he rushed over to the monitor for a closer look.

The image showed the rock formation where Bones had disappeared and Maddock had slid down the tunnel. The sun was bright and the picture was of high resolution. Two people were walking slowly around the formation.

One was some sort of law enforcement officer. Maddock figured probably a sheriff based on the hat. The identity of the other figure was what had made him rush to the monitor and now made his heart soar.

Angel!

Chapter 19

Alex Scano leaned back in his chair and closed his eyes. He shifted uncomfortably in his seat, the scars from his trek into the Maya underworld still paining him. Forcing the pain to a corner of his mind, he focused on the task at hand. One success and one... He hesitated to call it a failure, but Maddock and Bonebrake had managed to overcome the effects of the drug.

Not before they almost killed each other, though.

Scano licked his lips as he remembered watching that video. Unlike most of what the two men had seen in the cave, the combat between Maddock and Bonebrake had been real. A true test of the effectiveness of the planting of suggestions via virtual reality, whether it could make two best friends kill each other.

Scano frowned. His mistake may have been in assuming ScanoGen needed that sort of test. For all they knew, killing someone close might trigger areas of the brain not even impacted by the drug. He wasn't going to market it as creating perfect killers. In fact, he fully expected the primary customers to be groups which were already involved in violent conflicts and just needed to eliminate the problems which arose from sometimes unreliable recruits to their causes.

He had half a dozen groups ready to pay him as

soon as the product was ready. The most interesting was ISIL, which had some pretty savvy leaders despite espousing a return to the Dark Ages. They recognized that they couldn't create much of a caliphate without managing to enlist the support of the existing residents of cities and regions they had targeted for takeover.

So he wasn't worried about this latest setback. The only concern he had was that once again he had been unable to operate with full independence. That had proved disastrous in the Yucatan, but the only way he could continue to operate ScanoGen openly was to take on a partner with the influence to head off any sort of government attention. This partner required regular reports. He awaited the day when another of the products in the developmental pipeline would be complete and eliminate the need for the partnership.

Scano still hadn't settled on a final name for the finished product they were testing now. Internally they were calling it *Brainwash,* but to Scano that word evoked images of hypnosis or someone sticking needles in the brain. His product was much more refined and reliable. *Mind Bender* was one of the names he was considering. He liked *Reality Checker* as well, but his marketing people assured him that most customers didn't do irony.

His mind returned to the tests. As Renfield had noted, the real world test had been wildly successful. They'd gotten a highly ethical bank teller to steal a hundred grand with just a puff of vapor and a few sentences of verbal suggestion. The guy had snapped out of it within five minutes, but that was entirely predictable without the VR component.

That's what they needed, more real world tests. Once Maddock and Bones arrived and the scientists had analyzed their brains, he'd move on to the next phase. He'd already begun some careful infiltration around the edges of two of the biggest drug gangs in New York. Soon, his staff would be able to deliver to both gangs a dose of *Brainwash* and the VR along with it. Then they'd step back and see what happened.

In all honesty, he'd be doing the world a service. The rival gangs would almost certainly destroy each other with single-minded purpose, unconcerned with protecting their drug business. If the world were a just place, they'd give him a medal.

A knock sounded on the door.

"Come in."

His assistant walked in. Scano went through assistants like most people changed clothes, but this one had been with him nearly six weeks. Time enough to gain some confidence and not be afraid of saying something wrong with every sentence. This one was dark-haired with mocha skin, as were most of his assistants. He never mixed business with pleasure when it came to his staff, but a man couldn't be faulted for appreciating a certain type of beauty.

What was this one's name? Ah, right, Amy.

She was carrying a burlap sack, and she opened it to reveal a bunch of packages of hundred dollar bills. "What am I supposed to do with these?"

Scano stood and gazed down at her. His back still ached from the nerve damage he had suffered from contracting the ancient Mayan plague known as the *Shadow*. Only massive blood transfusions had kept him alive. "That's the money from the bank experiment?"

A look of mild distaste crossed his assistant's face briefly before she banished it. "The bank robbery, yes. Frank just brought it in and told me to give it to you."

"And you are giving it to me."

"Yes."

Scano knew he shouldn't toy with her, but he couldn't resist. "I don't want it."

"Excuse me?"

"I don't want that money. Frank shouldn't have given it to you."

She pondered that for a second. "So what do you want me to do?"

"Give it back."

"Give it back to Frank?"

"No, we're going to give it back to the bank."

"We're what? You robbed a bank just to give the money back?"

"We didn't rob a bank, Amy. We conducted an experiment, and an employee of the bank stole the money and gave some to us."

She seemed about to question that, but then stopped herself. "But why would you give the money back?"

Scano smiled and extended his hands palms up in front of him.

"Of course we'll give it back. What kind of a man do you think I am?"

Chapter 20

"**Angel!**"

Maddock launched himself out of the hidden door in the rock formation and sprinted the ten yards to his fiancée. Angel's shock at seeing him materialize out of nowhere lasted only half his run, and she closed the final two yards herself.

"Dane!"

After a few minutes of embrace, she pulled away slightly and looked up into his eyes. "Where have you been? And is my brother with you?"

Bones answered before Maddock could. "Of course I'm with him, saving his ass as usual."

"Bones! I'll never admit I said this, but I've been worried about you." She detached one arm from Maddock and gestured to Bones; then she noticed that Bones had his hand around the neck of a man walking in front of him.

"Sorry sis, a hug with you and Maddock at the same time is not the kind of three-way I'm into."

Angel scowled. "I take it back, I wasn't worried about you. But seriously, what happened to you guys?"

Sheriff Danzig's voice sounded. "I take it y'all have found each other?"

Bones and Maddock looked at the other man, who was offering a handshake.

"Sheriff Brad Danzig. Pretty sure I can figure out which one is Bonebrake and which is Maddock.

Who's the other fellow?"

Bones said, "This is Steve Renfield, security chief for the ScanoGen facility dedicated to testing their new drug, *Brainwash*."

Danzig narrowed his eyes and Maddock could see him making connections. "The facility wouldn't happen to be down that there hole y'all climbed out of, would it?"

Maddock nodded. "It is. How did you run into Angel? Thanks, by the way, for whatever help you've given."

Danzig explained his longstanding interest in the disappearances and Angel's arrival at his office that morning. Maddock and Bones went over what had happened to them since Maddock first received the text with the picture of a kidnapped Angel. Renfield remained silent, a glare on his face. By the end, both Angel and Danzig were shaking their heads.

"That's the craziest story I ever heard." Angel said.

Bones gave a snort of knowing laughter.

Angel ignored him. "I assume we're going after Scano?"

"Assuming our buddy Renfield here told us the truth about his location, then hell yeah."

Maddock looked at Danzig, trying to gauge the law officer's reaction to Bones' direct statement. Danzig's expression gave nothing away.

Renfield said, "I told the truth. But no

guarantees that he's there at any given moment."

Bones squeezed Renfield's upper arm and scapula together. "I'm sure we can find you again if he's not."

"What about them disappearances?" Danzig's voice wasn't loud, but it got everyone's attention.

Renfield blinked a couple of times but didn't answer. Danzig said to Maddock. "Your story explains every last thing about why folks kept turning up missing. But so far I ain't heard nothing about what happened to the ones before y'all."

Maddock turned back to Renfield. "How about it, Renfield, what happened?"

"Listen, I... Before I tell you anything more, I need some assurances. I have information to trade."

Bones slapped him behind the head. "Did I just hear him say he's been holding out on us? I've been wanting a new scalp for my trophy case."

Maddock said, "Renfield, you are not a smart man. A smart man would know when he's completely beaten."

"Like I told you before, Scano will go after my family."

Maddock opened his mouth, but Danzig beat him to a response. "What makes you think we won't?"

Bones guffawed. "You are so screwed Renfield. Even the law isn't going to play nice."

"You guys are worse than Scano. Fine, he targeted a bank yesterday. Stole at least fifty grand."

Maddock looked at Bones and Angel. "Fifty

grand is chump change to someone like Scano."

"It is. It was an experiment, just like what we did to you guys. He got an otherwise trustworthy bank teller to steal the money."

Bones said, "Don't know about the rest of you, but I couldn't give a crap about that. I want to find him."

Danzig's face had reddened over the previous minute, and now he lunged at Renfield and grabbed him by the lapel. His brown eyes flashed with tinges of orange. "Last time ah ask nicely. What did y'all do with those other folks?"

Renfield took a step backwards and tripped, winding up on his back on the ground. Moving with him, Danzig jerked him into a seated position almost before the fall was done. Renfield sighed.

"They're dead."

Danzig blinked and the hand holding Renfield's shirt started twitching. No one said a word for several seconds and then Renfield started yelling. "Did you hear me? They're dead. They're all dead. Scano took their brains and studied them so he could improve the VR process. Is that what you wanted to hear?"

A second later, the barrel of Danzig's Smith & Wesson was in Renfield's mouth. "No, son, it ain't exactly. You going to give me a reason not to pull this here trigger? Maybe your brain will be right useful for research if I spread it around."

Angel took a couple of cautious steps so she was near Renfield and within Danzig's field of vision. "Sheriff, I don't think you want to do this. None of us will say a word, but these things have a way of blowing back. This asshat isn't worth it."

Maddock felt a swell of pride at what Angel was doing but he tensed, hoping Danzig wasn't about to redirect his anger at her. The look the sheriff gave Angel wasn't angry, though. Maddock thought he had never seen eyes as haunted as Danzig's in that moment.

Danzig slowly withdrew the gun and got to his feet. Bones moved next to Renfield and once again clutched the back of the man's neck with a giant paw. Danzig holstered his gun, walked three steps, and then sank to the ground with his head in his hands.

Angel spoke softly. "You're not a killer, Sheriff."

Danzig looked up. "Maybe I should be." Then he took a deep, rasping breath. "That man murdered my baby girl."

Chapter 21

"**Talk to me,** Jimmy."

"I'll try, Bones, but you usually interrupt. Can you put Maddock on instead?"

Bones and Maddock had asked Jimmy Letson to look into the alleged bank robbery as well as the address that Renfield had given them. Letson had just called back.

"I'm hurt, Jimmy. The truth is that Maddock is all kissy face with my sister and can't come to the phone. Kind of makes me want to puke."

Letson chuckled on the other end of the phone. "Pay attention then. I researched that address in Maryland you gave me. It's an office park built about five years ago. It's small, with a huge wall and security gate so the general public can't nose around. And it's surrounded by a lot of old growth trees. I sent some info on the building layout to your phone."

"Aren't most office parks more visible? Companies want exposure."

"Yep. But you get this kind of thing around D.C. Often it has to do with government secrecy. Probably not in this case, though."

"Let me guess, it's owned by a shell company owned by ScanoGen."

"Not really. As usual, the chain of ownership is convoluted. In the end, it traces back to a Delaware corporation with Directors who include two high level individuals in the Turkish government."

"Turkey? What do they have to do with anything?"

"If I had to guess, I'd say they might be unaware of it. I got hold of images of the signatures on the incorporation documents and compared them with signatures of the officials in question. No match."

"Are we talking identity theft?"

"Hard to say. Maybe someone looking to embarrass Turkey or our government or both. All I can say for sure is that someone is engaging in misdirection."

"We could have figured that one out."

"Fine, then you don't need me to tell you what I found out about the robbery."

"Come on, man, don't play hard to get."

"You're an ass, you know that, Bones?"

"Have you been talking to Angel again? Come on, spill."

"The video confirms the story about the mist spray. There's no sound, so we have no idea what the guy said after spraying. But the cops aren't buying the teller's story."

Bones guffawed. "Hell, I can't blame 'em. I experienced it myself and I still wouldn't believe the story if I were a cop."

"That's not the oddest thing, though. This afternoon, the money reappeared. Someone walked in, dropped a sack of cash inside the door, then sprinted off down the street. Disappeared into an area without camera coverage."

"As dumb as that sounds, Renfield did say the robbery wasn't about the money. It was just a test."

"Sounds like a successful one. But I... Hold on, Bones."

Bones could hear what sounded like the television in the background. "Jimmy, if you're putting me on hold to watch reality TV, I'll kick your ass."

Jimmy's voice sounded subdued when it returned. "Bones, something just came on the news. An explosion just destroyed the Warren County Sheriff's office."

A rare chill crept up Bones' spine. "Hold on, Jimmy, let me get Maddock."

He knocked three times hard on the access door between the two adjoining motel rooms he and Maddock and Angel had reserved. Maddock and Angel had said they could all stay in one, but Bones had insisted that he did not want to be squeezed in the small space with the two of them. Maddock opened the door a second later. "Yeah?"

He held up the phone and activated the speaker function. "Maddock, it's Jimmy. There's been an explosion."

Jimmy's voice crackled. "There's information coming through on the news now. Sheriff Brad Danzig and an unnamed prisoner are presumed dead.

Maddock blinked. "Jesus. I'm assuming the prisoner was Renfield."

Bones said, "Gotta be. Any more details,

Jimmy?"

"Not at the moment. It just started hitting the web. Turn on the news and you'll know as much as I do."

They thanked Letson and hung up. Maddock called Angel in and told her what had happened. The news reports didn't really have any more information other than confirming that the origin of the explosion was in an official vehicle, but they watched anyway hoping for more.

Eventually Maddock hit the power button on the remote, which left the room dim in the late summer twilight.

"This sucks." Angel spoke first.

Bones grunted. "No kidding. Danzig was my kind of guy. That bastard Scano took them out."

"Absolutely he did, but no way we'll ever prove it." Maddock started pacing back and forth. After a moment, he raised his head again. "Screw proof. It's time to accelerate our plan to go after him."

Angel frowned. "Accelerate?"

"Yeah. Like tonight."

"Whoa." Bones lifted both hands. "Accelerate is one thing, reckless is another. We don't know anything about the Maryland facility. And, who knows if he's even there? With us escaping and killing the sheriff, he's probably lying low."

"Scano is an arrogant jerk. No way would he lie low in fear of us or anyone else. But we have someone who can help us get inside, someone who also hates Scano."

Bones sighed. "So we're going to owe Tam another favor?"

Tam Broderick ran a special unit within the CIA known as the Myrmidon Squad. It was so secret that even within the CIA few were aware of its existence. She had gotten her big break in the intelligence community working undercover in ScanoGen back when it had been run by Alex Scano's father Salvatore—a man who was every bit as ruthless as his psychotic offspring.

Maddock and Bones had worked with Tam on several Myrmidon missions in the past, and Tam's people had assisted Maddock and Bones on one or two occasions as well. She was fair, but never forgot a favor owed to her.

"Come on, Bones, life gets boring when we're not looking for alien gods or walking through the actual location of hell like we do when we're working for Tam. Besides, I already talked her. I called as soon as we got here."

"What did you tell her?"

"Everything. Well, mostly. She wasn't that interested until I told her he had a drug which could control minds. Since we know from Renfield that Scano is in the D.C. area, Tam said she could run a facial recognition search and see if he had shown up on the public camera networks. She's going to get back to us within the next hour."

"I'm impressed," Bones admitted. "And I suppose Tam will collect some favor to be named later, as usual?"

"Pretty much."

Chapter 22

Angel and Maddock sat down on Bones' bed. Angel took his hand. "I still can't believe it about Sheriff Danzig. Especially after what happened with his daughter."

Before they had left the sheriff, he had told them about his daughter's disappearance. Five years earlier, she had been last seen hiking by herself in the woods on the other side of the river from the park. At first Danzig had figured she just ran away for a time. The sixteen year-old was willful and in constant battle with her mother.

But some detailed research showed that far too many people disappeared within ten to fifteen miles of the park headquarters for it to be coincidence. Danzig began to suspect that a predator of the two-legged variety was using the area as a hunting ground. He had never suspected something like the secret ScanoGen lab.

Danzig said that aside from the girl's mother, they were the first people he'd told that the missing girl was his daughter. She was the result of one ill-advised night the summer after graduating from high school, and he didn't even know of the girl's existence until she was nearly ten years old. Both he and the mother kept it quiet, as folks in that part of Virginia still might frown on that sort of thing by an elected official.

That explained why Letson had found no

record of the sheriff's daughter being one of the missing. It also gave Maddock extra appreciation for the man's ability not to kill Renfield. Dark thoughts of his own wife—Melissa—who had died in an automobile accident, along with their unborn child, flashed into his brain, and he squeezed Angel's hand in an attempt to ward them off.

Against all odds, he had found happiness again, but he knew what grief could do to a man.

Tam Broderick called back in half an hour. Bones answered. "Chippendale's male escort service."

Maddock couldn't make out Tam's words, but he caught the tone of her voice—scolding like a middle school teacher correcting an unruly student.

After a moment, Bones held out the phone. "She wants to talk to you Maddock. I'm not sure why."

Maddock snatched it from him. "Yeah?"

"Did Bones tell you that you owe me another one?"

"He did, but since you want Scano as bad as we do I'm not sure I agree with that."

Tam chuckled. "We'll settle on something, we always do. You're in luck, we found Scano. He hasn't disguised himself and he doesn't seem to be avoiding public exposure."

"Seems pretty brazen for a guy wanted by a bunch of governments for terrorism."

"Maybe, but he probably owns a dozen legislators just in the U.S. I'd be surprised if he doesn't have people high up in the Agency and Bureau also. It's amazing what money will do."

"So where did you find him?"

"The guy regularly goes to a Starbucks in a suburban area in Maryland. The past two months, he's averaged three days a week there, always between seven and nine in the morning. Can't believe he would get into such a routine."

Maddock's pulse sped up. "He thinks he's untouchable. This wouldn't happen to be near the Shadow Creek Office Park, would it?"

He could hear Tam entering a few keystrokes. "Yeah, the closest one to that address." Her tone sharpened. "What do you know?"

"We were given that address by the guy we captured during our escape. He said it's where he met with Scano."

"And you didn't think to tell me this?"

"Information is almost as good a currency as favors," Maddock said.

"Good point."

"Something else just happened you should know about. Sheriff Danzig and probably Renfield were blown up in a car bomb an hour ago."

There was silence on the other end. Then: "Scano was behind that? This sounds like an urgent problem."

Maddock found himself nodding. "It is. And we plan on addressing it right away."

"What are you and Bonebrake cooking up?"

Maddock had given this a lot of thought in the

hours since their escape. "Scano controls information very tightly, so I doubt the information or any samples exist outside of a very small group. We get rid of Scano—cut the head off the snake—and the rest will be easy."

"Get rid of," Tam echoed. "I don't know if I like the sound of that. What about capturing him and getting him to talk?"

"We're happy to try. But Tam, you know the guy as well as anyone. What do you think the chances are of him allowing himself to be captured alive?"

Tam's sigh echoed through the line. "I should tell you to wait, to let my team liaise with you and plan an operation."

"You should, but you won't. Brainwash is some scary stuff. Scary as f—" He caught himself, knowing of Tam's strong aversion to profanity, and managed to substitute a euphemism. "Scary as heck. Scarier than just Alex Scano. We can't allow anyone to get hold of that, but how do you put that kind of genie back in the bottle? You're better off letting me and Bones deal with it as free agents." He didn't need to add that there were probably people in Tam's own agency who wouldn't mind getting their hands on Brainwash.

"I know better than to ask you to wait," Tam said, resignedly. "Just promise me you've given me all the information I need in case you fail and I have to clean up the mess."

"Fine. You can sign out some equipment

through the usual D.C. channel, but if you don't need anything else from me I'll sign off. I'll deny knowing anything about what you're going to do. But good luck doing it."

Maddock hung up and shared her information. Bones clapped his hands together. "Hot damn! I always wanted an Alex Scano punching bag. You want to go after him tonight?"

Maddock shook his head. "We know he's usually there in the morning. That's when we should go."

"Dude, there's something called daylight that will most definitely cramp our style if we wait."

"But he's not going to hang around there at night."

"Guys! Can I say something or do you two want to keep bickering?" Angel stood with her hands on her hips and her eyes flashing with anger. After hearing no response, she relaxed a fraction.

"As much as I hate having to say this, for once my brother may not have his head up his—"

"Hey!" Bones protested. She shot him a look.

"What's wrong with going there tonight? We don't have to actually break in or anything, just check things out. The more information we have before we actually confront him, the better. And there's one other thing."

"What's that, sis?"

"Do you really believe Tam is going to stay out of it?"

Bones raised his eyebrows and then chuckled.

"She's right, Maddock. Tam gave in too easily. She's got even more of a stick up her butt than you do when it comes to controlling operations. The sooner we do this, the less chance her people will be there and screw it up somehow."

Maddock met Angel's eyes. "Looks like I'm outvoted. Fine let's do it. But..." his voice trailed off.

Angel gritted her teeth. "Don't even think about it. I'm coming."

Maddock looked to Bones for help, but his friend just shrugged. An exaggerated sigh caused Angel to increase the intensity of her glare, but then Maddock embraced her.

"Of course you're coming. I just worry about you."

Angel squeezed him back. "I worry about you too, idiot."

Bones stuck a finger down his throat. "Unless you want to see my burrito again, get a room. Crap, you already got a room and it's right next door. Man, that's even worse. Forget I said anything."

As the hours ticked toward midnight, they prepared by looking at the diagrams Letson had sent them and going to pick up the equipment from Tam's supply location. Cramming in the rental car, they headed into Maryland.

Maddock looked at Bones, who was driving. "Is it me or does this feel a little different than most of our other adventures. When we find Alex Scano... We're going to kill him, right? I mean, he's not going to come in even if we threaten to kill him otherwise."

"I hear you, bro. Straight up murder isn't my style, either. But the good ol' boys used to have a saying back where we grew up."

"What was that?"

"Some folks just need killing."

Chapter 23

"**Looks quiet, Bones.**"

"Of course it is, Maddock, it's three in the morning. White people don't party this late."

Maddock, Bones, and Angel stood in the shadows of a parking lot across the street from the gate which served as the only entrance to the office compound in Maryland which Renfield had claimed was Alex Scano's headquarters location. Each wore an A/N-PSQ20 ENVG-III night-vision monocular covering the right eye. This new model of night vision optics, which could switch between infrared and thermal vision—or a hybrid of the two—with the flick of a switch, wasn't available yet even to most military personnel, but Tam Broderick had the contacts to provide it to her people.

The entrance gate was twenty feet high and constructed of thick cast iron. A brick guard house about fifty meters inside the gate contained an array of external lighting with enough lumens to disorient a blind man—and certainly bright enough to render their night-vision devices useless. At least half a dozen cameras were displayed in an overt show of security.

Angel said, "Forget the cameras, we're not getting through that gate even if we use Bones' thick skull as a battering ram."

"You're right, but I have other body parts that would do the trick."

Angel scoffed. "We'd need something much thicker to get that lock picked."

Maddock shook his head. "The gate's not the way to go. But I gotta say I'm surprised at the fence. That wall is over ten meters high and it goes all the way around the compound. So much for Scano lying low."

"Remember what Jimmy said, dude. It screams government. Everyone knows something is here, but there's no way to know what. Hey, maybe it's aliens!"

"Um, it's Alex Scano, remember?"

"Sure, but I just realized he could be an alien. That would explain a lot."

Maddock ignored him. "Obviously we have to get over the wall somewhere and scope out the place. We need to try to figure out if there are any gaps in the cameras."

"Don't forget motion sensors. We need to get back out before daylight, too." Angel added.

Bones removed a small tablet device from his backpack and powered it on.

He'd already set the brightness to a dull setting which was easy enough to see looking at it directly but didn't give off enough light to be spotted by someone more than a few feet away.

"I've been itching to give this baby a try," he said, as he removed a small machine from the pack and set it on the ground. About four inches tall, the mini drone—another piece of equipment supplied by Tam Broderick—contained ten rotors which allowed it tremendous maneuverability in the air. It was constructed of a material which both reduced its radar cross-section and absorbed the kind of minimal light common during the night hours. It would be as close to invisible as they could get.

Bones tapped the tablet screen and the rotors began spinning in near silence. The drone lifted off, and by the time it had risen fifteen feet in the air it had disappeared. Maddock and Angel looked at the tablet from either side of Bones. The drone contained six cameras, and the controlling app on the tablet used a complex computer algorithm to produce a detailed picture of the drone's view.

Soon the drone crested the wall to one side of the gate. Bones slowed it down, directing it along the top of the wall with about five feet of clearance. The layout stayed consistent as it went.

Maddock said. "Okay, looks like there are only cameras about every hundred feet or so. Lights every fifty feet. So far I haven't seen the cameras pointing up, so we can probably find a gap where we can drop quickly with minimal chance of being seen."

"Looks like a lip on the back side of the wall," Bones added. "The anchor should grab easily. We should do it around the side, though, in the park."

The parking lot they were in was accessible from two different parallel streets. They exited via the street a block away from the ScanoGen gate, to minimize any chance of being picked up by a camera. Then they made their way around to a small park which abutted one of the side walls of the ScanoGen complex. Bones had continued to run the drone, and its video confirmed that the camera and light layout remained the same on this other wall.

As they stood under some thick spruce trees, Bones brought the drone to a hover. "This looks like a good spot."

Maddock opened his pack and took out a fat coil of rope and the "gun" which would launch a collapsible grappling hook attached to the rope up and over the top of the wall. After a final check of the drone feed, he tilted the weapon up and depressed the trigger. The report of the compressed gas charge blasting the hook skyward wasn't nearly as loud as a gunshot, but was still loud enough to make Maddock wince. He remained stock still as the hook soared up, trailing out the rope like a spider's silk, then arced over the wall and dropped out of view. He stayed that way—completely motionless—for a full minute thereafter, eyes glue to the screen that displayed the drone feed.

Nothing. No alarms had been triggered. Nobody was coming to investigate the odd noise.

He turned to the others. As if by some mutual unspoken agreement, no one said a word. Bones flashed a thumb's up. Angel just nodded. Maddock returned the nod, and then clipped the gun to a carabiner attached to his heavy-duty rigger's belt. He depressed a switch on the gun's exterior, and activated its built-in motorized ascender. The device wasn't powerful enough to pull him straight up the rope, but it gave enough of an assist to make the job of "walking" up the wall like Batman and Robin in the old TV show, a little easier.

When he reached the top, he hooked one leg over before deactivating the ascender and letting it slide back down to Angel and Bones. Five minutes later, they were all perched atop the wall, and after repositioning the grappling hook, were ready to descend into the compound.

So far, so good, Maddock mused, but the thought brought more dread than comfort. When things went smoothly, it usually meant that bad luck was just around the corner.

With their ENVG's set to thermal—which would pick up on the body heat of roving guards and hopefully give them a few seconds of advanced warning—they made their way through the compound, following Jimmy's map. They didn't have an exact location for Scano. The man was a fugitive from justice after all, and unlikely to list his name or the address of his office within the complex. It was possible that he had staked a claim to one of the generic offices in the administration building, but Maddock's gut told him that, if Scano was on the premises, they would find him in the main research laboratory. Even if they didn't, the lab still would have topped his list for places to visit. He wasn't going to leave until he made sure Brainwash wouldn't ever be used against anyone, ever again.

They moved to a fire exit on the south side of the research building, the largest structure in the compound, and with the help of some remote digital wizardry courtesy of Jimmy Letson, succeeded in opening the door without triggering an alarm. They stole inside, and after another brief pause to ensure that they had not been detected, began moving down the corridors toward a cluster of rooms marked on the floor plan as laboratories #1, #2, and #3.

Maddock expected that they would have to proceed by trial and error, but they got lucky on their first try. The door to lab number three was locked, but a low hum of activity vibrated from it, and there was light streaming out through the crack above the threshold. Maddock used a digital "skeleton key" to override the card reader that controlled the lock, and when he heard the mechanism click, he and Bones swept inside, pistols leading. Angel, likewise armed with a Glock, would bring up the rear.

He cut right, knowing that Bones would go left, and began sweeping the room for targets. Anyone with a weapon would take first priority—he would shoot first and hold the questions for later. Everyone else would be dealt with on a case-by-case basis, but as far as he was concerned, anyone they might encounter was potentially hostile.

He saw no weapons... No security guards. There were only three people in the vast, mostly empty space of the lab, all of them clustered together around a lab table on the far side of the room with their backs to the door. Two of the figures were attired in white lab coats. The third wore a high-collared turtle-neck shirt. Even though Maddock couldn't see the man's face, he instantly knew that they had found their target.

"Scano!"

The three figures whirled around—the two men in lab coats immediately raising their hands in the air when they spied the guns aimed at them. Alex Scano looked like he might spontaneously combust from rage, but then his expression quickly transformed into a look of sardonic amusement.

"Well, well. Dane Maddock and the Bonehead twins. What a surprise." His voice was raspy, like someone with a two-pack a day cigarette habit.

"Sorry about the way things ended in Guatemala," Bones growled. "If we'd known you were still alive, we would've stuck around and put you out of our misery."

Scano uttered a terse laugh. "Maybe you should let Tiger Lily do the talking, Boner-brakes. She's actually kind of scary, unlike you two."

"You want to see scary little man?" Angel said, her voice as cold as steel.

Scano gave a mock shiver. "Ooh. See what I mean? You and Maddock are all bark, no bite. I saw the video from the Brainwash test. You two couldn't kill each other to save your own lives. No way are you going to kill me in cold blood."

The men in lab coats recoiled visibly at this

overt mention of murder. Maddock didn't think either one of them would pose much of a threat. He kept his pistol trained on Scano. "That's called being in control. Which is where we are right now. As for killing you… Well, we both know that you're about to do something stupid which will give us the excuse we need, so why don't you just get on with it. Make your move."

The mocking smile sharpened. "Let's talk about why you're really here. You want my little Golden Apple of Discord, don't you?"

"Cut the crap," Bones snarled. "There is no Golden Apple. Never was."

"God, you really are thick. It's called a metaphor." He threw his head back in a dramatic sigh, giving Maddock a glimpse of the angry scar tissue at his throat. "A rather clever one if I may say it. It's true, that story I told you about Franklin and King Louis was a contrivance. Our research suggested that the drug would work better if we provided a plausible rationale for the hallucinations. A Golden Apple full of chaos energy seemed like something the two of you would accept at face value."

"Guess again, pharmabozo," Bones countered. "We didn't buy it for a second."

Scano rolled his eyes and then waved his hand dismissively. "It doesn't matter. The point is, Brainwash *is* my Golden Apple. A little whiff of it, and you two were ready to kill each other. Now that's what I call chaos magic. It actually comes from Africa—a little place called the **Kundelungu Plateau**. I suppose Renfield told you all about it. I really should have terminated his employment a lot sooner. If there's one thing I can't abide, it's incompetence."

He sighed again. "But I digress. The natives there burn wood infiltrated with the fungus in fires to create a mildly hallucinogenic smoke which they use in their primitive rituals. We figured out a way to go 21st Century with it, and made it into vape juice, which is, let me just say, a helluva a lot more potent."

Maddock risked a quick glance over at Bones, and saw his own wariness reflected in his friend's expression. Scano was being unusually forthcoming with information.

He's stalling.

"We're still trying to isolate the exact chemical structure of the fungus so we can synthesize it, but for the time being, it's still cheaper to go to the source. And I'm sure that's what you're really here for, isn't it?"

"We're here for you," Maddock said, taking a step forward. "I promised a mutual friend that we'd try to bring you in alive. Whether you walk out or we carry you is another matter."

"See what I mean?" Scano made a barking sound, then half turned away, lowering one hand to gesture at the table behind him. "But seriously,

Brainwash is right here."

Maddock reflexively followed Scano's pointing figure to a small rack filled with stoppered test tubes resting on the table. In the instant that he looked, Scano made his move, slashing out with the extended arm to sweep the rack off the table, flinging it across the room toward Maddock and the others.

Even though he had been expecting Scano to make some kind of move, the suddenness of his action, coupled with the fact that Scano was still technically unarmed, caused Maddock to hesitate a fraction of a second too long. He shook it off and shifted his aim to track Scano, who was now darting toward a back exit, but before he could pull the trigger, the rack of test tubes crashed against the wall behind them, and suddenly they were engulfed in a pungent white cloud.

"Don't breathe it," Bones shouted, but Maddock knew it was already too late.

The mist dissipated but not quickly enough for Maddock to stop Scano from reaching the door. Cursing, he started forward, sprinting across the lab, intent on giving chase. He skidded to a stop in front of the door and yanked it open, but as he was about to step through, he saw that a sheet of solid steel now blocked his route.

He whirled around to face the door they had come in through, and saw Bones and Angel contemplating a similar barrier there.

Scano had triggered some kind of security or safety isolation protocol. They were locked in.

"Damn it," he rasped, mentally chiding himself for not having anticipated something like this.

Angel uttered a low wail that was completely out of character for her. She had turned and was backing away from the door as if it had suddenly become red hot.

"Oh, my God. It's closing in… The walls." She spun in place, looking at the far wall behind them, and then turned to Maddock. "They're closing in. We'll be crushed."

"Crap," Bones muttered. "She's right."

Maddock saw it, too. The walls were sliding toward them, encroaching inch by relentless inch, forcing them back….

He bumped into something… Turned and saw a lab table piled with scientific apparatus. It hadn't been there a moment before, but in the instant it had taken him to confirm that the walls were indeed moving inward, the lab tables had slid away from the walls, clustering in the center of the room to form a devilish maze.

He dropped to his hands and knees, intent on scuttling underneath them, but as he started forward into the forest of table legs, he saw writhing shapes hanging down from the underside of the tables like the tentacles of a Portuguese Man o'war.

"What the…" He recoiled, scrambling back until he bumped into the moving wall.

This couldn't be happening. Isolation doors

were one thing, but the rest of it? It was like something from a nightmare….

Realization broke through the Brainwash-induced fugue like sunlight slicing through the fog. "It's not real," he muttered. "Not real."

He wanted to believe it, but the tables and the wriggling tentacles told him otherwise.

If you can't trust your eyes…

But his eyes *were* deceiving him. There were no tentacles. The walls weren't moving to crush them. It was all a hallucination. Angel had unwittingly planted the suggestion in his head, and the drug had done the rest.

"It's not real," he shouted, rising once more to his feet.

As if the words had magic power, the maze of tables shimmered and vanished, clearing his path to Bones and Angel. Bones was staring back at him with a glimmer of understanding, but Angel looked positively freaked out. She was backing away from the wall, her head bobbing left and right as if surrounded by snakes.

For a moment, Maddock thought he could actually see a nest of vipers all around her, but he knew that they existed only in his head.

"Angel! It's not real. It's Brainwash."

She swung her gaze around to meet his, but unlike Bones, there was no gleam of comprehension in her eyes. "Who are you?" she snarled, and brought her Glock up, aiming at him. "What have you done with Dane?"

"Angel, it's me."

He could see her finger tightening on the trigger. She was going to shoot him.

That's not Angel.

The idea bubbled up like swamp gas in his brain.

It's not her. Scano replaced her with a look-a-like. It's a clone... No, a shapeshifter. It killed Angel, and it's going to kill me if I don't....

His gun was up and trained on her before he knew what he was doing.

"Maddock," Bones shouted. "Angel. Put your guns down. This isn't real."

The words broke the spell for Maddock, but Angel was beyond their reach. She swiveled the gun toward her brother, the fear in her eyes doubling. Bones let his own pistol fall, raising his hands in a show of surrender. "Sis, it's me," he pleaded, and then, perhaps sensing that a different tack was called for, sharpened his tone. "Don't be an assclown. Put the damn gun down."

There wasn't even a flicker of recognition. She was going to pull the trigger. She was going to shoot her brother, and then she was going to shoot Maddock.

Unless I shoot her first.

No! It's Angel!

It's not Angel.

But it was, and she was in the grip of a

hallucination that would kill them all if he didn't somehow find a way to wake her up.

Hallucination.

An idea struck him. Angel's claustrophobic hallucination had been contagious because Brainwash made them all susceptible to the power of suggestion. What if he could use that to distract her, get her to point the gun somewhere else.

"Angel!" He barked. "It's me. Dane. Look at me."

She turned both her eyes and her gun to him.

Slowly, so as not to spook her, he pivoted, aiming the gun at the wall to her right, and said, "Shoot them."

Angel's head snapped around, her eyes going wide as her drug-addled imagination filled in the blanks, and then the business end of the Glock followed. The pistol thundered, then thundered again and again, shifting a few degrees with each discharge. Maddock had no idea what she was shooting at—the bullets were simply gouging holes in the very-much motionless walls—but he knew he had bought only a brief reprieve at best. He had to get the gun away from her somehow, wake her up....

As if in answer to his unspoken prayer, Bones closed with Angel, wrapping his arms around hers, sweeping down to brace her forearms against her hips to prevent her from aiming the pistol at either of them. A swat of his powerful right hand knocked the pistol from her grasp.

Against anyone else, that might have been the end of the fight, but Angel wasn't anyone else. Faster than Maddock's eyes could follow, Angel twisted in her brother's embrace, lashing her fists up into his unprotected face. The fury of the attack forced Bones to let go, and as he staggered back, she pounced.

Bones was quick for his size, but Angel was lightning-fast. She snapped a sharp jab that caught Bones on the bridge of the nose, followed with a kick to the knee that nearly toppled him, and then danced out of his reach. Bones shook his head and moved forward.

"Angel, calm down," Maddock urged, moving closer. "Both of you. It's the drug. The Brainwash. You have to fight it, not each other."

Bones made a quick move, grabbing for Angel's wrist, but once again she was too fast. She sprang to the side and punched him in the elbow.

"Are you freaking kidding?" Bones snarled.

Angel feinted a right cross, but Bones wasn't biting. He saw the next punch coming, a left to the ribs, let it land with a dull thud, and quickly trapped her arm against his side.

Now drawn in close, Angel lashed out with an elbow strike that Bones took on the side of his head. It was a vicious blow, but the man had a thick skull. Angel tried to break loose, and almost succeeded, but Bones grabbed her wrist with both hands.

Angel leapt into the air and attempted a

roundhouse kick to the head. It was a measure of her mental state that she tried such a crazy attack.

It didn't work.

Bones turned and ducked. Simultaneously he pulled Angel off-balance. Having left her feet, it was easy for the big man to take her down. She landed hard on her back, but immediately kicked out, with both feet, catching her brother on the shin.

He cursed and grabbed her by the ankle, and she made him pay by driving her heel into his chin. Momentarily stunned, Bones lost his grip, allowing Angel to roll away and regain her feet.

"You're fighting out of your weight class," Bones said, stalking her.

Maddock wracked his brain, trying to think of a way he could bring this to an end. At the start, Bones had been merely trying to subdue Angel, but with the Brainwash still in his system, there was no telling how far this would go. He had to stop them before they killed each other, but putting himself in between a pair of angry Bonebrakes wasn't the answer.

"Angel, you've got to listen to me," he said. "You're not yourself."

But Angel didn't hear. Bones had her cornered, and she lashed out with a fury. Her punches came lightning-fast, but Bones managed to dodge or block most of them.

"Don't make me knock your ass out."

Maddock could tell that, sister or not, his friend was on the verge of doing something drastic. He was going to have to intervene, but on who's side?

Frantic, he looked around for something he could use to distract them, and then his roaming eyes noticed something, not on the tables or on the floor, but on the ceiling, directly above them.

Will that do the trick? He wondered, and then decided that he had to take the chance.

In one smooth motion, he snapped his pistol up and fired once.

The bullet blew apart the glass bulb of an overhead fire-suppression sprinkler, instantly releasing a torrent of murky water that rained down like the Flood.

The water splashed down on Bones and Angel. For a few seconds, neither of the combatants seemed to take note, but as the chilly water finally soaked them through and sluiced away the last few grains of Brainwash that were still in their nostrils, the figurative fire of their mutual rage guttered and died. They both retreated a few steps, away from the incessant artificial downpour, and regarded each other with more confusion than animosity.

Maddock ventured closer. "Guys, are you with me again?"

Bones nodded. Angel just looked at him, bewildered. "What the hell just happened?"

"Scano happened," Maddock replied. "And he's getting away."

He glanced back at the door through which their foe had fled, and wasn't at all surprised to see that it stood wide open. The steel barrier had been just one more illusion conjured up by Brainwash.

Bones blinked as if trying to clear his head, then said, "If he's outside, I might be able to pick him up on the drone."

"Try it," Maddock said, "But do it on the move if you can."

He stepped closer to Angel and reached out with a tentative hand to touch her shoulder. She still looked a little rattled from the fight with Bones—the reasons for it had probably already slipped from her mind—but she placed her hand atop his and gave it a squeeze. "I'm good. Let's move."

They headed through the back exit and were on their way to another fire door when a blaring siren assaulted their eardrums.

Angel yelled to be heard above the noise. "Is that because you shot the sprinkler?"

Maddock could only shrug. "Must be on a delay," he shouted back. "Let's get outside."

But leaving the building brought only a measure of relief. The sirens were blaring all over the compound, lights flashing every couple of seconds, alternating red, orange and white light. Even stranger, there were people streaming from the buildings—researchers in lab coats, security guards in uniforms, workmen and janitors. Many appeared to be on the verge of panic. None of them paid any attention to the bedraggled looking trio standing in the shadows of the research building.

Maddock began to get a tingle in the back of his

neck, something which occasionally happened when he started to sense an unexpected complication. He had a feeling that they weren't going to like whatever was behind this development.

"Anyone have a clue what's going on?" Angel asked.

Bones said, "If I had any less of a clue I'd be a politician."

"I think we need to get out of here," Maddock said. "We'll try to pick up Scano's trail once we're back over the wall."

The alarms and flashing lights continued unabated, but as the evacuation dwindled, they made a run for the back of the compound, where they used the grappling gun to scale the wall again. Once on the other side and secreted in the trees of the park, Bones flew the drone to the front gate to observe the gathering crowd.

"Hey, check that out." Maddock pointed to the tablet. Three maintenance vans had just arrived near the gate, each with a Spark Energy logo and a natural gas symbol on its side.

"A gas leak? Come on, does anyone actually fall for that?" Bones muttered.

"Gas leaks do happen," Angel said, "But this is a hell of a coincidence."

Maddock still felt the tingle in his neck and was trying to hear what his subconscious was telling him. "Maybe Scano cooked this up to distract everyone while he slipped out."

"I—" Bones stopped as a tremendous boom

sounded and then rumbling shook the ground beneath them. Maddock's right foot slipped on some leaves and he fell to the ground. Bones clicked his tongue.

"Not very smooth, Maddock."

Maddock bit back a response then stood up and looked over at the tablet screen. The feed from the drone now showed only static. Bones started swiping a finger back and forth across it.

"The drone is spinning. I can't get it back under control."

Angel and Maddock watched as Bones continued to work the tablet. After a minute, he let out a breath. "Okay, I think I have it back. We're still near the gate, about fifty feet off the ground."

The feed was beginning to clear, and it became apparent that what they had assumed was static was in fact smoke. Maddock gasped as the pictures became distinct enough to make out the scene on the ground, a scene which had him blinking to make sure his eyes weren't deceiving him.

The building which had formerly constituted the ScanoGen research lab was nothing but a smoldering pile of rubble.

Chapter 24

"**Tying up loose** ends." Maddock muttered under his breath.

"What?"

Maddock looked at Bones. "Scano is tying up loose ends. First the car bomb that killed Danzig and Renfield. Now his headquarters is gone."

Bones raised his eyebrows. "I guess the guy's got a thing for blowing stuff up. If you're right, he'll probably disappear again."

Angel said, "That, plus he must already have backup plans for *Brainwash.* This sucks on multiple levels."

Bones gritted his teeth. "All I know is that it sounds like I don't get to pound on him."

Over an hour had passed since the explosion, and the first glimmers of dawn were spreading across the sky. The three of them had retreated a couple of blocks away to avoid getting caught in the law enforcement activity which had begun shortly after the blast. Sitting in the rental car with the ENVGs wasn't completely secure, but Maddock wasn't about to walk away yet.

He flipped the goggles back over his eyes. At this point only the bomb squad truck and fire vehicles had been allowed beyond the gate, and a perimeter of police tape separated a bunch of other official vehicles and personnel from a small but growing crowd of onlookers.

A figure caught his attention and he increased the magnification to take a closer look.

"That's him."

Scano appeared to be having a discussion with one of the uniformed officers manning the perimeter. Maddock studied the man's features with whitening knuckles.

"No way, dude. Is he really that stupid?" Bones flipped down his goggles. "I guess he is."

"What the hell's he still doing here?"

Angel looked as well. "I assume we're not going to march over there and say hello. Should we call Tam?"

Maddock and Bones exchanged a look before Maddock allowed a wry smile. "Who says we can't march over there and say hello?"

"But..." She met Maddock's eyes. "You guys are not completely sane, you realize that?"

Bones chuckled and opened the car door. "Sanity is overrated. But in this case we're just curious members of the public. Everyone loves an accident."

When they reached the scene a minute later, Scano's argument with the officer had escalated into a shouting match, accompanied by numerous expressive gestures from the ScanoGen leader. Maddock could see a couple of other officers starting to shift in the direction of the confrontation, hands sliding down toward their holsters.

"I'm the owner of this complex and I demand to know what's going on."

"Sir, I'm not going to tell you this again. Not only is this an active crime scene, we also haven't confirmed that it is free of additional threats. No one is going in there except emergency personnel."

"Take me to your supervisor. I'll deal with someone who can make decisions."

"Sir, I'd be happy to give you my supervisor's phone number. But I warn you that she has even less tolerance for self-important blowhards than I do."

Scano's face reddened. "I'll have your badge, officer."

The police officer sighed. "This is D.C. If I had a dime for every time someone's said that to me, I'd be on my private jet right now. Do you want her phone number or not?"

Bones and Maddock picked that moment to approach from either side of Scano. Angel hung back a few feet. Bones put an arm around Scano's shoulder.

"Alex, buddy! Are you making things difficult for the cops again? You know better than that. Shame about what happened to your building."

Scano's eyes showed a second of calculation, then he pointed at Maddock. "Officer, these men had something to do with the explosion. You need to arrest them!"

The police officer rolled his eyes. "First you tell me you'll have my badge, now you want me to arrest your friends. If we weren't so busy here, you'd be the one getting arrested."

"But—"

Bones smiled at the policeman. "I'm sorry about Alex, officer. He's a good guy, but when he heard about the explosion he rushed out here without taking his meds. He'll feel bad later about treating you this way."

Before the police officer could answer, Bones exerted enough pressure on Scano to turn him around. Scano bent his knees and dug in his heels, but Bones hissed in his ear.

"After the performance you just gave, I could drag you by your eyeballs and the cop would just shrug and be glad you were gone. So the amount of pain I cause is up to you."

Scano closed his eyes and relaxed his body. After they had moved ten feet away, Bones squeezed the bones of his arm hard enough for ligaments to start separating. Scano yelped, and Bones grinned. "Okay, maybe not totally up to you."

As soon as they reached the sidewalk, Maddock stepped in front of Scano. "Okay. Tell us everything about Brainwash, including any place where it is stored."

Scano scoffed. "Or what? You'll let me go? Even if you torture me, you'll never know if I told you everything. I survived a plague that wiped out an entire civilization, I think I can take whatever Chief Bonehead here can dish out."

Bones' features darkened. "Soft guy like you, I

won't even have to break a sweat."

"So do it. You already blew up my facility, see if you can beat me."

Maddock tried not to show his surprise at learning that Scano wasn't the one behind the explosion. "Hate to break it to you, but that wasn't us."

"Wasn't you? Come on, I..." Scano clearly read something in Maddock's eyes that indicated the he wasn't lying. "If it wasn't you, who was it?"

A voice from behind Maddock surprised everyone.

"It was me."

Suddenly it all made sense. Maddock turned to face the newcomer, who was accompanied by half a dozen members of her team.

"Tam."

Tam Broderick acknowledged him with a brief tilt of the head. "Maddock, Bones, thanks for getting Scano. Saves us having to extract him from the cops."

Maddock noted that Tam and her crew wore FBI hats despite the fact that they had nothing to do with the Bureau. "I see you came prepared for that. But why the charade? Why tell us we could go after him just for you to pre-empt us?"

Tam held up her hands. "It's complicated. Let's just say additional information came to our attention shortly after we spoke.

Bones said, "So you decided to blow up the complex? I can't believe you get all the fun."

"Believe it, big man. We can take it from here. Boys?"

Several of her team took Scano from Bones, with another one fixing handcuffs behind his back. Maddock grabbed Tam's shoulder before she walked away.

"You've pretty much always been straight with us. I don't know what's so important that you're willing to throw that away now. But whatever we owed you for getting us the info on Scano is gone. I can't imagine we'd trust you again. So I hope it was worth it."

Tam turned back to him with a look in her brown eyes approaching pity. "Maddock, there are things going on that are way above your pay grade."

Bones chuckled. "Spare me. We've found Atlantis, Noah's Ark, and aliens who gave technology to ancient man. No way pharma bro here is all that."

Tam glared at him. "Nevertheless, I am taking Scano. Now."

She turned and left with her crew, who had stopped and watched the interchange with obvious curiosity. Maddock wanted to do something to stop her, but he couldn't think of a single thing. At least not anything productive. He felt a soft hand on his shoulder.

"Dane. It's okay. Tam will make him pay."

Maddock closed his eyes and allowed a slow exhale. "Something's off. She didn't even say a word about the VR technology. Blowing up the building doesn't eliminate that threat."

Bones grunted. "Whatever's going on has her spooked. I've never seen that look of fear in her eyes other than a couple times when we were under attack."

"So what do we do now, Bones? Just let it go?"

Bones spread his palms. "I wanted to hammer him as much as anyone, but unless we want to take on Tam and the CIA then yeah. We let it go."

Maddock turned to Angel, who smiled and nodded. He rubbed his eyes with his hands. "I can't believe Bones was the voice of reason."

"Hey, it happened a couple other times recently. Angel must be a bad influence on you."

Angel punched him in the shoulder. "Asshat."

Bones rubbed the spot where she had struck. "That smarted."

"Don't be a baby. I was using my left."

Maddock's burner phone rang and he answered it.

"Maddock."

"Maddock, it's Corey."

Corey Dean was the only member of Maddock's crew with no military experience, and he served as the expert in all things technical. "Hey buddy, how's the R&R going?"

"Relaxing. You still coming back in two days?"

Maddock had forgotten that the original week of vacation was almost over. Time flies when you're trapped in a cave with VR in your head. "Probably. It's been ... interesting. Why, what's up?"

"If you're saying it's been interesting, my guess it'll be at least a three beer story."

"Maybe six."

"Cool. Well I'm just calling because we got a message from a potential client. Salvage of a wreck from the early twentieth century, one supposedly with a lot of gold bars. They want an answer by tomorrow."

"I don't know, Corey. After the last few years, it's hard to get excited about a ship full of gold."

"Did I mention that the wreck is haunted? The last three companies to dive on it have disappeared without a trace."

Maddock's eyebrows went up. "That sounds more like it. Give me the guy's number and I'll work something out."

After hanging up, he gave the news to Bones and Angel. Bones said, "Works for me. Unlike you, I'm fine with the gold too."

"Guess we better see about a flight home. It still burns me to let this thing with Scano go."

Bones put an arm around his shoulder.

"Don't worry, Maddock. One of these days, Tam will need us again. And when she does, we'll have just what every former SEAL turned hunter of lost treasures wants."

"What's that?"

Bones showed all his teeth. "Leverage."

EPILOGUE

Alex Scano had waited in the room with no lights and no human contact for three days. The room contained a single bed in one corner, and a toilet and a sink in another. He was only aware of this fact because he had been given ten minutes to memorize the layout when he first arrived.

The walls were smooth concrete, with no windows and not even any electrical outlets. Scano had noticed the hum of an air conditioner sending forth cool air from the vent in the ceiling twelve feet above. Food was delivered to him three times a day, and he had begun to obsess about the thirty seconds of dim light which shone through the small slot in the door during those times. He had called out every time, but no one ever answered.

The food deliveries were the only way he knew that three days had passed. He knew what his captors were doing. It didn't take much sensory deprivation to make most people frayed balls of anxiety. Scano knew it was starting to work on him, but he resisted it by doing mental exercises after every meal.

Sooner or later, Tam Broderick would regret this. Sooner or later, she would be made to pay. She had no idea what kind of influence Scano's partner had. Scano would just have to suck it up until that happened.

When the door opened, the dazzling light

nearly blinded him. A male voice barked an order. "On the bed."

Scano crawled over to the bed and lay on his side, blinking to get his eyes to adjust. The man held a gun and remained at the door, but another figure was approaching him. She carried a folding metal chair, which she opened and sat on a few feet from the bed.

"Tam. Nice of you to finally join me."

"I can't say the same, Scano. I was otherwise occupied. If it were up to me, the waterboarding would have started the minute we got you here."

"Ah, so you're not in control of the situation. I had a feeling that might happen. So when do you let me go?"

Tam smiled, her white teeth contrasting against her brown skin in the dim light. "I think you may be operating under some sort of misimpression. No one's ever letting you go."

The first tendrils of doubt seeped into Scano's brain, but he pushed them aside. "Brave talk, but I think we both know how this will end."

Tam shook her head. "Deluded to the last. Let's just start with the questions, shall we?"

Questions he could handle. Scano gestured with an open palm. "Fire away."

Tam made a triangle in front of her with her two hands. "Hmm, should I start with an easy one? Nah, I think you can handle the good stuff right away."

She moved the chair closer and leaned so that

her face was nearly over the mattress.

"Tell me about your arrangement with the President."

The End

About the Authors

David Wood is the author of the Dane Maddock Adventures and several other titles. Under his David Debord pen name he is the author of The Absent Gods fantasy series. When not writing, he co-hosts the Wood On Words podcast. He and his family live in Santa Fe, New Mexico. Visit him online at www.davidwoodweb.com.

Edward G. Talbot is the pen name for the collaboration of two authors: Ed Parrot and Jason Derrig. They have created a brand of thriller that keeps the stakes high while not taking itself too seriously. How do two people write a book without killing each other? That's easy. They don't own any weapons and they stink at unarmed combat.